SHADOWLAND

JT Grossmith

SHADOWLAND

Copyright @ 2024 by JT Grossmith.

All rights reserved.

Printed in the United States of America.

No part of this book may be used or reproduced in any manner whatsoever without permission except in the case of brief quotations embodied in critical articles and reviews.

A stanza from the T.S. Eliot poem *Gerontion*;

a couplet from Robert Frost, *The Road Not Taken*.

This work of fiction is based largely on actual events. All of the characters identified by name and position existed during the story's timeframe. A list of the principal characters is available at the back of the book. Except for those instances indicated by quotation marks, all of the dialogue attributed to each character is fictional.

The author acknowledges that this work would not have been possible without the research efforts of numerous non-fiction authors, most notably, Seymour M. Hersh and his definitive work,
The Dark Side of Camelot.

Table of Contents

Prologue i

1960...1

1961...15

1962...76

1963... 130

1964... 195

Postcript 233

Principal Characters.................................... 235

About the Author 237

Prologue

My identity is not important, but I am one of the few people with any real understanding of the man known variously as The Kingfisher, the Gray Ghost, the Black Knight, the Orchard Man, the Fisherman, Jesus, Slim Jim, Skinny Jim or Scarecrow in the gray circles or the Shadowland, as we thought of our universe. Clearly, the multitude of nicknames suggests, at the very least, a confused or complex view of his true persona. Half-American, half-Hispanic, his father served with General John 'Black Jack' Pershing in the campaign against the revolutionary leader Pancho Villa. He subsequently married a woman of Mexican descent, Carmen Mercedes Morano. She gave James Angleton his middle name of Jesus. Over time, the Kingfisher et al. became a ghost of a man whose files rivaled those of J. Edgar Hoover for having the goods on people, particularly the seamier side of their lives.

At his zenith, he was considered to be the Company's equivalent of the Delphic Oracle, reflecting the notion of one who exudes wisdom in all things. In reality, well before the end of his career, he had become a parody of that character. Once erudite, tall, and angular, as he aged and the events of the times took an increasing toll, he became noticeably stooped, almost cadaverous in appearance, his fingers stained yellow from years of heavy smoking and his entire body often reeking of alcohol, a result of his prolific consumption of wine and spirits.

It was commonplace in that era for people in the organization, and those whose paths we regularly crossed, to indulge themselves during lunches and dinners. Some people like James Jesus Angleton believed that they were immune to the effects of copious drinks, but that was only an illusion. I don't know whether it is the drink, the hoarded secrets that always weighed heavily on their minds, or some combination of both, but like others in the service, he became so caught up in the paranoia of their trade and the labyrinth of secrecy that had been constructed during that period, that it became increasingly difficult for him to distinguish between reality and illusion.

Over time, he never opened the blinds in his office, and somehow convinced those in the agency with the authority to allow it, to build him a safe that occupied several rooms and which only he had access to. Not even his superiors had a key or authorization to enter it. Increasingly, Angleton spent hours and days on end in the safe, sifting through his papers, trying to piece together the clues that would reveal the identities of Soviet moles, who he believed had gained prominence in the country and whose common goal was to undermine the security of the United States of America. In the end, he became so reclusive that people in responsible positions were incapable of recognizing him, even if he was standing beside them in an elevator.

1960

The voice is youthful yet confident, albeit one with a distinctive New England accent.

"In 1933, Franklin Roosevelt said in his inaugural that this generation of Americans has a rendezvous with destiny. I think our generation of Americans has the same rendezvous. The question now is: Can freedom be maintained under the most severe attack it has ever known? I think it can, and I think, in the final analysis, it depends upon what we do here. I think it's time America started moving again."

In any other political forum during an American presidential election year, such a statement might be greeted with loud and sustained applause, but given the venue of a television studio, there is little more than an eerie silence as the Junior Senator from Massachusetts, John F. Kennedy, completes his opening remarks on this late September day in the first-ever political debate to be carried on television.

It has been predicted that there will be somewhere close to 70 million Americans watching this historic occasion. Yet, we are all, in a sense, very much alone or limited to whatever small group can squeeze into the family living room or wherever the television set is located.

I am sitting with my mentor, the head of counter-intelligence at the CIA, James Jesus Angleton, whose attention, for the most part, appears to be elsewhere, ruffling through files, constantly withdrawing and then returning them to their proper place in his attaché case. Smoke from an ever-present cigarette curls around his head and drifts in and out of my line of sight of the TV picture.

It can be distracting at the best of times, but tonight, I am managing to ignore it as I concentrate on the flickering black-and-white images dancing across the screen. As the evening progresses, one thing that is increasingly evident to me is that there is a clear distinction between the two central characters. Even the degraded images of this still-developing medium cannot camouflage the obvious differences in physical appearance between the individuals who are making history on it.

John Fitzgerald Kennedy appears tanned and extremely fit — vigorous and robust as they might say in New England — while his slumping, ashen-faced opponent seems to be dissolving before our very eyes into his dark, five-o'clock shadow.

Strange, I think, for a man who hails from California, the land of perpetual sunshine, but then darkness has been the trademark of Richard Milhous Nixon throughout his career, and nothing that he says, or the manner in which he is saying it tonight, gives lie to that lingering perception.

Kennedy is just killing Nixon, don't you think? I ask of my companion.

Funny, it doesn't sound that way, JJ replies, projecting a line of thought that some newspapers and observers will elucidate in the days to follow.

But you're not watching, I counter.

No, I prefer to listen so that I can concentrate on what is being said.

I suppose I shouldn't be surprised. It is apparent to me, and others have mentioned it as well, that JJ or the Kingfisher as he is often referred to in the trade, albeit never to his face, is less enamored of Kennedy than many who are rallying to his campaign as the election nears its due date.

I have been receiving disquieting intel about his campaign, he tells me after the TV is turned off.

Disquieting?

More than simply that. You know about West Virginia?

Only that the Kennedys spent a lot of money in the primary there to defeat Humphrey, I respond.

JJ smiles.

Spent is a bit of an understatement, wouldn't you say?

I simply shrug my shoulders.

Bribed would be more accurate. We figure that the Junior Senator from Massachusetts spent countless millions of old Joe Kennedy's ill-gotten gains to pay off county sheriffs and other local officials necessary to make sure that they delivered the vote for him in sufficient numbers, effectively putting an end to Hubert Horatio Humphrey Jr.'s Democratic nomination ambitions.

I haven't seen those reports, I respond. Are they ours or the FBI?

Well, you know they have to be FBI for the most part.

And that doesn't concern you?

It might under normal circumstances, but consider this: How else do you explain a Catholic defeating a Protestant in West Virginia? It defies logic.

I ponder for the moment the implications of money buying Protestant votes in an America that historically has not embraced Catholics with presidential aspirations.

Not just Protestant votes in West Virginia, he adds.

That statement catches me off-guard.

Joe Kennedy is also negotiating with the mob to ensure that Chicago and Illinois are in the right column come election day. And there may be other states in play as well.

The mob?

Joe has lots of connections in that regard.

So do you, I'm told.

JJ chuckles softly.

Now where would you hear that?

I've heard things…about your time in the underground in Italy…fighting the Nazis during the war with the help of certain Italian factions.

You can't believe everything you hear.

No, but certain things seem to add up.

Again, JJ chuckles, this time a little more heartily.

You are learning, he allows.

Okay, so what's the Chicago story? I ask.

Joe Kennedy is dealing with a guy there, whose name, ironically, is Humphreys — Murray Humphreys.

That doesn't sound much like a mob name.

JJ smiles.

It doesn't, and that probably works for him because he's the front man for Sam Giancana, the guy who controls most of the action there.

And you have connections with Sam! It's more of a statement than a question.

JJ just shakes his head wearily.

Time for you to go, he says, returning to his papers.

JJ invites me to spend the weekend at his home, Casa Nogales, in McLean, Virginia. I expect his wife, Cicely, is away at one of her family residences, probably Tucson, although no explanation regarding her absence is forthcoming from JJ.

Saturday is spent in his private greenhouse tending to one of his personal passions: Orchids.

Much of our conversation, albeit one-sided, is foreign to me as JJ carries on a running commentary on the pollinating conditions for Cattleyas, Oncidium, and other varieties of orchids, and how they relate to our trade.

Orchids are not like most species, he explains, where only the fittest survive. For these delicate beauties, survival depends upon each one's ability to deceive.

How's that? I ask, interrupting the master somewhat inappropriately.

His eyebrows arch, owlish eyes narrow behind oversized glasses, and his large, sensuous mouth tightens. But the tension passes as quickly as it arrived.

Take this one, for example, he says, picking up one of the numerous plants in the greenhouse. What do you see?

I don't know, I answer awkwardly. They are all very beautiful, but aside from color...

My response trails off into what remains of the late fall sunshine.

Fortunately, JJ jumps into the breach. Deception can come in many ways: Color, shape, even odor is used to mimic characteristics that appeal to insects which are necessary for pollination and, hence, he pauses for effect, propagation. This particular beauty appeals to me because it relies on sexuality.

I know better than to speak, thereby transmitting my sense of disbelief, but by now, JJ is so engrossed in the specimen he is holding that even my visual clues are missed.

It may not be apparent to you, but it perfectly mimics the underside of a female fly, right down to the hairs and odor, he says assuredly.

It is all I can do to stifle a laugh.

A passing male fly is deceived into believing that there is a female fly here for the taking, and not unlike most males of species, JJ intones, he immediately has only one thing on his mind — to have his way with it. The clinical term as to what transpires is pseudo-copulation, but the result is very real because he becomes an unwitting carrier when he strikes the pollen pod. Hence, the process of propagation is perpetuated.

The mere prospect of such evokes a huge smile from JJ.

Fortunately, a fly has no memory of unfulfilled sex, and so, he repeats the process with the next orchid that he passes, and pollination ensues.

The same is true in our craft. It's not always a question of obtaining information about what our enemies are about but rather deceiving them into thinking about what we are doing. Unfortunately, he allows, it is not quite as simple a process as it is for orchids.

Think of it, he continues, the number of orchid species is constantly growing and now possibly exceeds the number of mammal species by an order of four and boasts about twice as many as birds.

Now, only one or two successes of this magnitude would suffice for us. But orchids are not JJ's only non-office interests. It is said that he is an avid collector of semi-precious gems, many of them from the Southwest, an important part of his heritage despite the image he projects of being an English gentleman, right down to the bespoke Savile Row suits he favors and a black wool Victorian Homburg.

Then, there is his fascination with fly-fishing, particularly in the company of one Sam Pepich, a tall, tough Serb from Butte, Montana, who, prior to joining the FBI, worked in the copper mines like his father before him. Now, he serves unofficially as JJ's liaison man, having done so for the past 10 years. Papich likens their outdoor experiences to fishing for spies. JJ, he has told me, walks a portion of the river he plans to fish, inspecting the water, vegetation, and insects before fashioning his flies. Papich says JJ could expound on the life of the mayfly, from the larval stage up until the time it's a fly, which doesn't surprise me, given the detailed explanations he imparted to me on orchids.

Nonetheless, he never keeps the fish he has caught as it is the challenge of catching them, not unlike the challenge of catching spies. It is understood, however, that spies will be kept. To his many admirers, fly fishing and orchid nurturing were not accidental interests, but rather extensions of the skills he considers to be a requisite for any successful counterintelligence officer.

Not surprisingly, time passes despite allegations about how the president's victory in Illinois, critical to winning the election, was achieved. To keep myself occupied, I have begun immersing myself in the nuances of the Trust and the Rote Kapelle, both of which transpired some 40 years ago in the Soviet Union and, as best as I can determine, have virtually no bearing whatsoever on the current world situation. Nonetheless, these two examples of Soviet lore are something, I have been told by the likes of Raymond Rocca, Scotty Miler, and others with close associations to JJ, that I must study for precisely eleven years, not ten, nor twelve, if I am to be of any value in the department. It's all supposedly part of learning the intricacies of the black arts, of which JJ is considered a masterful player.

As its name implies, the black arts utilize a variety of techniques, such as propaganda or playback, to facilitate disinformation. In the case of the Trust, the idea was to lure dissidents living abroad in the Twenties back to Russia under the mistaken assumption that they would be protected and would be able to work more effectively in the pursuit of changing the regime. In reality, they were all rounded up, eventually, one by one, and executed. If there is a lesson to be learned from the Trust, I suppose it is that if you can persuade your opponents that you are on their side, then it will be much easier to manipulate them in the future if the need arises.

Whether it would take eleven, much less ten or twelve years, to learn this and other subtleties of the Trust and Rote Kapelle is not immediately obvious.

Nonetheless, disinformation is not the sole objective of JJ's operations. When circumstances warrant it, he has bugged the phones and residences of high-ranking U.S. government officials and foreign dignitaries, all with the approval of our director of operations, Allen Welsh Dulles, albeit over the objections of various deputy directors of operations, who ostensibly JJ is supposed to report to during his years of service. But it is well-known that if the situation calls for it, JJ is not averse to circumventing proper channels to acquire personal data on anyone within the Company or other agencies, activities that are clearly outside of our charter and violate FBI jurisdictions. Officially, he has access to everyone's personnel, operational and communications files, even Dulles', which at times has strained their personal relationship. Still, our director values the information that JJ is capable of obtaining, even if it occasionally casts him in a less-than-desirable light.

I am told by reliable sources that JJ once had a bug planted in the pillow of one of our media operatives, Thomas Braden, which provided a transcript of pillow talk between Braden and his wife, Joan, that included some disparaging remarks about Dulles.

Allen decided, in effect, to confront Braden.

"You'd better watch out," he warned Braden. "Jimmy's got his eye on you."

Braden said he drew the obvious conclusion: JJ had bugged his home and was picking up personal conversations between himself and his wife. Interestingly, Braden said he was only mildly surprised at the incident, because JJ was known to have bugs all over town.

I, too, am not surprised by such revelations, given that I have been with JJ many mornings when he would enter Allen's office to report the take from those overnight taps. Allen was always delighted with stories of what happened at people's dinner parties and other less-public occasions, provided they didn't involve him. All of the reports are done in the guise of fishing talk. The moment JJ enters the office, Allen would inquire: 'How's the fishing?' And JJ would respond: 'Well, I got a few nibbles last night.'

Because JJ keeps the most vital and sensitive files to himself, he has become a storehouse of secrets that have helped consolidate his power base.

But fishing talk, the Trust, and Rote Kapelle aside, thankfully, JJ has other plans for me at the moment, and I am summoned into the inner sanctuary for an update on the current political situation.

I suppose you were happy with the results? JJ asks while sorting through some files in his office. Your boy won. In fact, I never thought I'd see the day when someone could outfox 'Tricky Dick' in the manner that he did.

He chuckles genially and lights a cigarette before continuing.

I suppose Nixon never had a chance once Kennedy trotted out his line about there being a missile gap between us and the Soviets. Everyone always thought of Nixon as the cold-war warrior, and here's this young upstart claiming, in effect, that Dick and Ike had been asleep at the switch for the past eight years.

I nod in agreement, having reflected some on that very same thought.

And then, during that final debate, JJ continues, he applied the coup de grâce, announcing that his administration would liberate Cuba.

Were you listening, he asks me, or still just watching?

I was listening as well as watching, I reply, adding, you couldn't help but see that Nixon looked like he'd been hit in the face when Kennedy dropped that bomb.

Kicked in the balls might be more accurate, JJ says matter-of-factly. Nixon knew that we were working up to something, but he couldn't say so because he felt obligated not to talk about top-secret plans that he was privy to as a member of the Eisenhower administration.

Then, to add insult to injury, Allen decides that we should put our plans to knock off Castro on hold because, being a Republican and an acquaintance of Nixon, it would look like we were playing favorites.

Not to change the subject, I interject, but do you think Kennedy will keep Allen on as head of the Agency?

A sliver of concern momentarily crosses JJ's face.

I suppose our new president owes him that for not having done anything to disrupt the election, but, you know, Allen is a Republican, and his brother John Foster Dulles held the office of secretary of state during this past administration. Those are not ties that one can build on.

I nod in agreement and then remember his earlier shot at me.

By the way, I add somewhat defensively, I never said Kennedy was my boy.

It certainly sounded that way when you were watching the debate, he responds, digging even deeper into my sensitivities.

I was just observing what I was seeing on the TV.

Well, let me tell you what we've been observing, he says.

You've been watching Kennedy?

It wouldn't be prudent to depend entirely on the good will of the FBI once the possibility emerged of him becoming a president.

What good will — have I been missing something?

JJ ignores my remark and continues.

I don't know how much of this works its way down to people like you, but our newly elected president is a busy boy, and I don't mean just politics.

Busy?

During his California swing, JJ continues, you know when he got that tan which made him look so much better on TV during the debates, he also found time to dabble in some of the local talent, particularly, a Judith Campbell.

I haven't heard of her.

That's not surprising, but what is…

He pauses momentarily to reflect on what he is about to divulge.

What's surprising is that she is also frequently seen in the company of Sam Giancana.

I thought Giancana had his hands full with that singer, Phyllis McGuire.

JJ nodded.

No denying that, but Sam, like our new president, is not one to limit his relationships, but I'm not so sure he is as successful with Campbell as he would like to be. They meet a lot, but not in a manner that Sam might prefer.

My confusion shows.

It would seem that the lovely Judith, JJ continues, is acting as a go-between or a runner, in addition to keeping our new president satisfied.

Runner?

Ah, huh. She's been observed, on several occasions, delivering what we suspect are cash payments to Giancana.

As you predicted, I ventured.

Well, the Illinois results were very interesting. Kennedy suddenly pulling enough votes in Chicago to overcome his downstate disadvantage. Hell, even Adelai Stevenson failed to carry Illinois in his two campaigns against Ike, and he was the damn Governor.

But how do you know that she's delivering a payoff? I ask.

Well, on one occasion, the FBI managed to have her followed.

Oh?

It wasn't difficult. After a tryst with the president-elect in Washington, she boarded an overnight train to Chicago, carrying a satchel that she didn't have in her possession until she met up with lover-boy.

And she went on her own?

That's what she thought, but in fact, she was being shadowed the whole way by one of Kennedy's advance men, a Martin Underwood, who kept her in his sights until she turned the satchel over to Giancana.

Must have been important, wouldn't you think? he asks.

And this was at Kennedy's direction?

No, I expect it was Kenny O'Donnell, his close friend and special advisor, who sent Underwood along.

Unbelievable!

JJ just nods.

And I fear that's not the end of it.

Just before the holiday season commences, JJ invites me over for drinks and, surprisingly, what at first appears to be idle chit-chat.

After more than a couple of whiskeys, JJ leans back in his chair, eyes closed, and confides in me: You know, the Kennedys are notorious for the secrets that they keep hidden in the closet.

I look at him blankly.

Starting with the president's maternal grandfather, 'Honey Fitz,' a corrupt Boston mayor, and their father, the Kennedy boys quickly learned that they lived a privileged life and often, as a result, were not going to be held accountable for their transgressions.

Oh, that sounds religious.

Now that you put it in that context, you are aware that the president's marriage is not his first?

What?

JJ chuckles before quickly turning deadly serious.

The president, in typically brash and irresponsible behavior, married a Palm Beach socialite, Durie Malcolm, back in 1947 when he was just a first-term congressman. Within days, the marriage collapsed. I suppose you could think it was simply more of the president's unquenchable appetite for sex. Nonetheless, it was left to one of his oldest friends, Charles Spalding, to clean things up, including collecting all the wedding documents a few days after the nuptials. No divorce was needed, hence his ability in the future to be married in the Catholic Church.

Oh, my. Does Hoover know about this?

Again, that draws a humorous response.

Of course he does, JJ says with an uncharacteristic grin.

1961

Before you let yourself believe
what you want to believe,
you must inform yourself what it is,
that it is necessary to know.

There's more than just a cold, biting wind hurtling down Pennsylvania Avenue on January 20th as a coatless and hatless thirty-fifth president takes his oath of office.

JJ has wheedled an invitation to observe the ceremonies on TV from the comfort of the exclusive F Street Club, where a group of senior military officials grimly watch as the president speaks, following his swearing-in.

I am there as well to observe the mood.

In contrast to his cool appearance on TV during the debate, Kennedy appears to be sweating profusely despite the frigid conditions.

This is not lost on one of our party, Eisenhower's retiring physician, who becomes increasingly animated as the speech wears on.

"He's all hopped up," General Howard Snyder finally exclaims at one point, referring to the sweat accumulating on the president's brow.

Everybody turns to him.

He's on medication, the good doctor explains.

How do you know? asks Admiral Arthur Radford, a former chairman of the Joint Chiefs.

The doctor hesitates momentarily, recognizing that he is about to divulge confidential information, but then these are his peers, so he continues.

He gets a shot of cortisone each morning, among other things.

For what? Radford wonders.

Addison's disease.

There is silence as this startling piece of information sinks in.

But Dr. Snyder's not finished.

His personal physician, he's referred to as Dr. Feel-Good, is constantly giving him…

Dr. Feel-Good? one of the military men interjects.

Max Jacobson, Dr. Snyder answers and continues.

He must have given him an extra shot today to help him deal with the stress of the situation.

They are treating him for all manner of conditions never associated with someone of his status and position — gonorrhea, syphilis — you name it. I imagine our new first lady has also been infected.

Everyone stands in shocked silence as Dr. Snyder gulps down the remainder of his drink.

I hate to think of what might happen if our new president is required to make a decision on national security at 3 a.m., he adds, shaking his head as he walks away.

We all return to watching the TV in stunned silence as JFK intones what many consider to be the trademark of his administration:

"Ask not what your country can do for you — ask what you can do for your country."

I bet more than a few ladies are going to be thinking about that when they meet the president, JJ whispers in a quick aside to me as we head to the bar for yet another refill.

We are standing outside of JJ's suite when we see Allen Dulles shuffling down the hall towards us in sockless slippers, no less, a sure sign that he is suffering from yet another bout in his recurrent struggle with gout. Slippers aside, Dulles presents a curious picture at the best of times, favoring old tweeds with patches at the elbows, a bow tie, bright glasses, a precisely trimmed mustache, and the ever-present corncob pipe. Whereas, JJ, like most of his colleagues, leans towards dark suits featuring a thin pinstripe.

Also, like most, cigarettes are JJ's preferred source of nicotine, although his particular choice often raises an eyebrow at first encounters as he has a fondness for Virginia Slims, a brand designed for women and marketed with the slogan: *"You've come a long ways, baby."*

The ultra-length, narrow smoke — only 23 mm in circumference and upwards to 36 mm, longer than conventional cigarettes — often seems to be little more than a prop, protruding from JJ's mouth at a raffish angle. Although one is constantly lit, more often than not it is ignored and allowed to burn to the point that the cigarette shape is transformed into an elongated ash, before finally capitulating to the law of gravity and crumbling onto a desk, file, his lap, or whatever else is handy.

Personal idiosyncrasies aside, Dulles and JJ have a long-standing relationship that has withstood regime changes and all manner of ticklish situations. But the recent election seems to be signaling a new era and with it the possibility of the kind of change neither man is willing or capable of embracing.

Dulles takes a few drags on the pipe while lighting. JJ has yet another cigarette on the go. I cough once or twice as smoke fills the room, but neither seems aware of me or my increasing inability to breathe. Not for the first or last time is the irony lost on me, that two of our arguably fiercest Cold War warriors seem to spend as much time battling their nicotine habit as they do waging war against our foes.

Finally, Allen is satisfied and turns his attention our way. It appears that I may have made a bit of a mistake, Jim, a couple of weeks back.

Oh, no, no, Allen, JJ counters, that's not possible.

Dulles sighs deeply. Hubris, my boy, hubris.

JJ is amused.

Hubris, Allen, oh, my.

Dulles ignores JJ's flippant remark.

I was at Walter Lipmann's a few weeks back.

One of his salons, Allen?

Yes, there were a few of us there: Cord Meyer, Richard Bissell, and William Bundy. Drinks, dinner, conversation. All of it off the record, of course, although Walter always finds a way to weave information he gathers from these gatherings into his column or it at least puts him onto people who will talk for publication, whether there's attribution or not.

Well, I can't say that I have noticed anything in Lipmann's columns of late that would cause you such distress, Allen, JJ responds while stubbing out the remains of his cigarette in an ashtray. His hand shakes momentarily.

No, that's not the problem, Dulles allows.

We wait as he sets to work again on his pipe.

Well, he finally continues, looking increasingly distressed, Bissell starts talking about how excited he is to be working with the Kennedys, ahhh because our new president is surrounded by a group of men who have a much greater awareness than the outgoing administration did of the extreme crisis that we are living in. Something like that, you know Richard.

Yes, JJ agrees, drawing on yet another cigarette, something like that, I suppose.

Anyway, Richard carries on to the effect that he doesn't think they will be inhibited about trying to do something about it.

Like Cuba, perhaps? JJ wonders aloud.

Dulles nods in agreement.

In Richard's mind, that's for sure.

So, JJ shrugs, what's the problem?

Dulles starts and then stops while he works yet again with the tobacco in his pipe before puffing a few times satisfactorily.

Yes, Allen, JJ prompts.

Dulles picks at his words carefully.

I forget who it was…but someone asked me my opinion of the new gang and…I suppose I was a bit condescending in my response.

Oh, really, Allen, you, condescending?

Now don't be a smart ass, Jim.

So, what did you say, Allen?

Dulles lets out an exaggerated sigh. My recollection is that I said something to the effect that I didn't really see much reason for concern and that, in fact, and I probably used these exact words: "I was continuing to follow the policies of the past administration."

Who knows? I may have even mentioned my brother in that context.

JJ tries to stifle a laugh but ends up coughing violently for what seems like an eternity. Finally, he regains his breath,

I suppose a little discretion might have been in order, Allen; after all, the last thing the new president wants to be seen doing is following in the footsteps of the great John Foster Dulles.

Allen is less than amused and shows it.

Thank you, Jim, I knew I could count on you for understanding…

But Allen, I don't see the problem JJ starts, and then it's as if a light has gone on.

Unless, of course, this has somehow gotten back to our new fearless leader or one of his minions.

I'm afraid it has, Allen says resignedly.

Bill Walton was there.

The fag artist? Oh, my, JJ responds.

Oh, yes, Allen allows. As you know, there's a certain affinity between Joe and Bill. Nothing we want to discuss at any length for sure, but Bill's also the dear friend and great companion of both our new president and his lovely wife.

Hmm, JJ ponders. I suppose it could be a concern.

Allen nods.

It's already starting to work its way down the line that the president is not too happy about my comments and that I had better be more mindful of who my new boss is if I expect to continue in my present station.

Oh, it's all just bluster, Allen, JJ declares, attempting to reassure him. The president wouldn't dare try to replace you, much less Hoover, for that matter. He's too inexperienced, and the press would crucify him.

I agree he won't try and get rid of both Hoover and myself, Jim.

For one thing, Hoover's got too much on him and his old man.

Ah, the famous Hoover files.

Yes, Hoover and his files.

Maybe we need more of those kinds of files ourselves, Allen?

That's what I was thinking, Jim. More fishing expeditions…something along the lines of those you've shown me from time to time when some of our leading citizens and statesmen here in Washington are acting in a less than appropriate fashion…you know.

But they only just amused you in the past.

Well, this is not a time for amusement, Jim! Damn it all, these are critical times, and to have the fate of our nation resting on the shoulders of a neophyte, well…

He grimaces and bites down hard on the stem of his pipe.

…We can't have him bringing in his own band of amateurs to provide the kind of guidance that our more practiced hands are accustomed to doing!

Besides…

He pauses, grimacing once again in a most unusual manner for the typically sedate Dulles. We've still got this Cuban thing hanging fire.

I know, JJ says, frowning. Any news on that front?

We're starting to have some preliminary discussions. More bringing him and his brother, Bobby, up to speed on the situation.

I thought he already had an appreciation for the situation from before the election. It certainly appeared that way every time he spoke on the issue during the campaign…

Only the broad strokes, Jim. Now we are starting to fill in between the lines.

And how is that going?

Well, I don't know that I share Richard's optimism to be frank about it, Dulles states.

How's that?

It's not what he's saying but what he's not saying.

Richard?

No, no, the president.

JJ stares at Dulles, imploring him to continue, but the old man returns to fixing his pipe.

Finally, after what seems like an eternity, involving much filling and tamping down of tobacco and fiddling with his lighter, the pipe is back in working order, and Dulles continues.

The president is gung-ho on ridding us of Castro, he says between puffs. After all, he said as much during the election.

Yes, yes, we know that, JJ responds with noticeable agitation.

Dulles, seemingly oblivious, plows on.

But it's the manner in which he wants it accomplished

that's worrisome. I'm getting the impression that he expects it to be a clandestine operation. At least no obvious connection, ah, in a manner so that it can't be linked directly to us or his administration.

Oh, really, JJ responds. Richard is saying this?

No, no, that's a problem, as well. Richard is not reporting this to me.

He's your boy, Allen.

You're all my boys, Jim.

You know what I mean, Allen. He's your replacement.

Dulles is not about to concede that point, but JJ continues to stare at him until he finally waves him off.

He's one of several I would consider, Jim, including you.

JJ laughs, momentarily breaking the growing tension in the room.

Allen, I have no illusions about me succeeding you if and when you leave. Maybe Helms, but certainly not me, Allen. No, not me.

Have it your way, Jim. Regardless, the people I'm hearing from about this lack of commitment to the operation are those who are at the meetings with Richard but are getting a different take on the situation.

And is that the message going down the line on this, Allen?

No, it isn't Jim. I'm afraid Richard's enthusiasm, shall we say, remains the order of the day.

And what about the Pentagon, Allen, what's their take?

They appear to be equally deluded, thinking that everything's a go

A go?

Well, not exactly in those words, Jim, but yes, they believe that once the operation starts, there will be no opportunity for the president to waver, much less back-peddle.

But surely, they recognize from what you are telling me…is…that there's no commitment?

I wouldn't say that, Jim. They equate wanting Castro out of there with authorizing the use of our armed forces and other resources once events come into play. They are preparing air missions and readying their naval options.

Does the president know this? JJ asks.

Both men stare at each other.

Good question, Dulles finally acknowledges. I don't think that he or his staff are sufficiently up to speed to understand exactly how things transpire from our end of things or the military's once the process begins.

Has he been advised about the Czechoslovakian shipment of arms to Cuba?

Yes, Dulles replies. The Joint Chiefs, ahh, General Lemnitzer, briefed him on that development right after he took office. In fact, if I understand it correctly, the general told him in no uncertain terms that because of this increased military buildup, deposing Castro could not be done in a clandestine fashion, and that we would have to expand our support operations in that regard.

And what was the president's response to all of this, Allen?

At the time, we thought he recognized what it will take to get rid of Castro.

Now?

Now, I'm not sure.

JJ's not finished.

What about the airport in Latin America that we poured

several millions into last year so that we have a foreign site to launch or cover any action?

Dulles shrugs.

The Swan radio network?

Again, there's no response from Dulles, just a worried look.

Damn it, Allen, we've put a lot of resources into the programming, the ads — all that stuff directed at undermining the Cuban people's support of the Castro regime.

He's been briefed on all this stuff, Dulles finally replies. I talked to him last August, before the election, for about two or three hours at the family compound in Hyannis Port and again during the transition period in January before the inauguration.

What about the hit-and-run attacks that have been ongoing since last spring?

All on the record, Dulles replies.

Howard Hunt's mission?

By this point, Dulles is beginning to show signs of exasperation although it's not clear entirely as to whether it's with his pipe or the continued line of questioning.

And? JJ demands.

And that's the problem, damn it, the president and his boys think it all supports their notion that this operation can be carried off without having any overt, much less official, U.S. connection.

I'm telling you, Jim, all I hear from them and our people, Richard aside, is this obsession with having Castro taken out without direct military involvement.

By whom? JJ asks.

They don't really seem to care whether its Cuban ex-pats,

Castro's own people, or the Mob, Dulles replies.

JJ's not satisfied.

It just doesn't follow, Allen.

He pauses to marshal his thoughts before continuing.

You could claim that Kennedy won the last election on the Cuba issue. He raised it in the debates last October and even criticized Ike, arguing that if you can't stand up to Castro, how can you confront Khrushchev? And now you're telling me he wants it done in a manner where he won't be seen as the instigator, much less get any credit?

JJ's on a roll but Dulles is having no part of it and starts to leave.

We better cover our asses, Allen, JJ calls out to the retreating figure.

The door closes.

A few days later, there's another meeting with Dulles, but this time in his office. Clearly, the situation is evolving in a disturbing fashion. There have been ongoing meetings with the president and his key advisors to present different scenarios.

What's the latest on Cuba? JJ asks.

Richard and I met with the president yesterday at 4:15, to be precise, and presented him with three alternative plans for the Cuban operation, Dulles begins.

JJ quickly interrupts the boss.

Have all of these plans been vetted by the military?

Dulles rolls his eyes.

Of course, Jim, we keep them totally informed.

JJ's eyes widen.

Totally informed?

Dulles sighs deeply.

You know what I mean, Jim.

Both men are distracted momentarily as they attend to their respective sources of nicotine.

After a few attempts to relight his pipe, Dulles puts it down in disgust and speaks in a staccato manner, which is completely out of character for him.

The first option is a modification of the Trinidad Plan, the second targets an area on the northeast coast, and the third is the Zapata Plan, which I believe you are more familiar with, Jim.

The Bay of Pigs landing, JJ responds.

Right.

And…

The president appears to be favoring the third plan, providing we make some modifications. He thinks it will look more like an inside guerilla-style operation.

Oh, right, fits in with this new clandestine obsession…. Then what?

Richard sent Jim Noble to Miami to put it to the exile leadership.

Put what?

That they need to get their act together. They've got to be unified because the burden will be on them…

And this was, where?

Dulles seems momentarily perplexed by JJ's insistence on learning all of the minutia involved.

At the Skyways Motel, he says, waving his unlit pipe.

So, they pulled together something?

The Consejo Revolucionano Cubano.

That's a mouthful…

This is more than a mouthful, Jim.

And what about the military? JJ asks.

The chairman of the Joint Chiefs…, Dulles begins

Lemnitzer!

Dulles nods, then proceeds to tell him that the general has informed Admiral Dennison of the requirements for naval support of the operation and that, at this point, they are talking about having one destroyer accompany the landing craft to about three miles offshore, where a landing ship dock will deliver the personnel, supplies, and transportation to the shore. All of it to be covered by U.S. naval air. But, Dulles notes, after pausing to regroup, Dennison wants to know if we can respond to attacks from the Cubans during the transfer process.

And can we? JJ jumps in.

After some contemplation, Dulles merely shrugs his shoulders.

I don't know. It depends on who you talk to and when you talk to them.

How's that?

It's in a state of flux.

So, when do you think it's going to be resolved, one way or another?

First of the month, maybe.

A smirk covers JJ's face.

Oh, April first?

Dulles is not amused.

Nonetheless, there is increased activity.

Word circulates that all parties have reached a compromise on air support for the Zapata plan, involving limited air strikes to be carried out two days prior to the invasion, but in a manner that will leave the impression that they are being undertaken by Cuban pilots defecting from the Cuban air force.

The Joint Chiefs of Staff are lukewarm at best about this proposal. They think it shows indecision or, worse still, a lack of commitment.

Yet, it appears to be going forward. Or is it?

Not content to question Dulles about the coming Cuba invasion plans, JJ hooks up with Bissell in between his sessions with the White House.

"Do you have an escape hatch?" he inquires of our lead man, "in case the thing falls flat on its face. Is there someone who goes to Castro and says, 'you have won the battle. What is your price?'"

A look of incredulity crosses Bissell's face.

There will be no failure, he assures JJ.

That's what I feared you would say, JJ responds.

Bissell shakes his head and walks away.

Back from another liquid lunch, JJ corners Dulles in his office to get an update, entering through the side door that is his usual access point, refusing initially even to sit down.

I'm hearing some disturbing, or at least conflicting reports, Allen.

Now, what are you hearing, Jim? Dulles responds wearily.

That the president is still polling his advisors and that McNamara wants the Joint Chiefs to reconsider the rules of engagement.

Yes, I suppose there's ongoing consultation. Would you expect anything else?

JJ starts pacing the floor, puffing furiously on yet another Virginia Slims.

Consultation, I suppose, but everybody around him is either a bootlicker or a pacifist…

Dulles appears to be absorbed with his pipe, so JJ carries on.

…Sorenson registered as a conscientious objector in 1948 when there wasn't even a war on.

The poet Robert Lowell…

You're fond of poets, Jim, Dulles interjects. You are always quoting Frost, Eliot, and that other fellow, Ezra….

…Ezra Pound, Allen, but none served time in prison during the war as a conscientious objector like Lowell or fills the head of the president with nonsense like Sorenson and Schlesinger.

These are the people that are important to him, Dulles begins but is quickly interrupted by JJ.

You know, Jackie hates Ted Sorenson.

Dulles appears to be momentarily confused.

What do the feelings of the president's wife about a speechwriter have to do with this issue, he says, shaking his head.

Besides, I don't think he's consulting Sorenson in this case, but I agree that Schlesinger has been extremely vocal on the matter.

JJ sits down, pulls out a crumpled package of cigarettes, and lights yet another one. After a few drags, he continues.

Sorensen, Schlesinger, it matters a great deal when we have these kinds of people offering advice on the logistics of a military operation.

Dulles shakes his head wearily.

Tell me, Allen, what expert advice did Schlesinger give to the president?

It appears you already know, Jim.

I want to hear it from you, Allen.

Dulles relents.

Something to the effect, Jim, that the invasion force is not strong enough to topple Castro.

Of course, it isn't, JJ affirms, shaking his head.

And how did the president respond to this news?

A smile begins to form briefly at the corners of Dulles' mouth, then disappears as quickly as it started.

Apparently, the president told him not to worry because he had reserved the right to stop the action as late as 24 hours before it is launched.

Damn it all, JJ exclaims, looking up at the ceiling, I imagine that raised a few eyebrows over at the Pentagon.

Oh, of course it has, Jim, Dulles says while getting out of his chair.

Look, we can talk about this later. Right now, I've got people coming in.

But JJ is not leaving without the last word.

I've talked to Richard about whether he has an escape hatch.

How's that, Jim?

In case this thing falls flat on its face…which, increasingly, appears to be a likely prospect.

Dulles begins to laugh nervously.

JJ's intense stare stops him.

I don't think the president wants us to be concentrating on fallback plans in the event this all falls apart, Dulles finally concedes.

But that fails to satisfy JJ.

You know, I can never quite figure you out, Allen, he says as he heads for the door. Are you the man who built this agency, ignored presidential directives when you deemed it necessary, and was not afraid to use unseemly material against those who would oppose us? Or, he pauses for effect, are you, at heart, still just the son of a Presbyterian minister?

Dulles sits down, lights his pipe, and reflects on that thought for a moment.

I suppose I'm a little of both, he says, pausing. I expect that disappoints you somewhat, Jim.

What was that all about? I ask JJ when we get back to his office.

We had a little program in the Fifties called Operation Paperclip, he begins, which facilitated the relocation of a number of Nazi scientists from Germany to here in America.

And there was a problem with that? I ask.

Very much so, JJ replies. It was a political non-starter. In many cases, it involved finding a means to obscure their histories and, in some, even short-circuiting efforts to bring their backgrounds to light.

Okay, so that doesn't seem to be that out of place for the

times.

It wouldn't have been, except that both Truman and Eisenhower issued presidential directives to the effect that such practices should stop.

And we ignored them?

Allen did.

The look on my face elicits a further response from JJ. We all have difficult decisions to make from time to time.

But ignoring a presidential directive? I reply.

We occupy a different landscape than the politicians, JJ responds. He lights a cigarette before continuing, For appearances' sake, they must maintain the pretense of operating in the sunlight, leaving us to do their dirty work in the shadows, if you will.

But, but…I stutter.

Don't you understand? It is simply inconceivable that a secret intelligence arm of the nation would be expected to comply with the overt orders of the government that are designed solely to mollify the public.

At that point, he starts shuffling files, in effect dismissing me.

The situation is deteriorating by the hour. Now, there is talk in the halls that Richard Helms has interjected himself into the issue, arguing at length with Bissell in support of non-military involvement. The big question is whether he has conveyed his position to contacts at the White House. People start to choose sides, but Dulles, in a rare sign of authority of late, attempts to put a stop to it by declaring that Richard

Bissell, not Richard Helms, represents us in discussions with the administration on Cuba. But with such division both here and at the White House, it's inevitable that the press gets wind of what's happening.

JJ slaps down a copy of the *New York Times* on my desk containing a page one story about the invasion.

He laughs.

Apparently, the president is lamenting that Cuba doesn't need spies. It only needs to read U.S. newspapers.

And that's funny? I ask.

Well, he snorts, that's kind of obvious, isn't it? This is probably the only thing that the Joint Chiefs of Staff and we agree with the president on…And it doesn't stop there.

There's more?

Oh, yes. Recent reconnaissance flights estimate that Cuba has 36 planes, more than originally anticipated…

So?

The White House, in a magnanimous move, has increased the proposed air support to eight planes from six.

He looks at me with a rare, mischievous twinkle in his eyes.

I don't know how the Joint Chiefs are managing to constrain their joy.

I have some news, I tell him.

Two of the operation sub-commanders met with Bissell and threatened to resign because of the ongoing changes to the plan.

Did they, now? JJ muses.

It didn't have much of an impact, I continue. I guess Bissell told them we're going forward with or without them, and they reluctantly agreed to stay on.

Do you think Helms has been working the Cubans? JJ asks.

That would be my guess, I respond.

As the operation's date approaches, the game of chicken continues between the White House, and us and the military.

In an effort to force the administration's hand, Task Force Chief Jake Esterline sends an emergency cable to Nicaragua enquiring whether there has been any change in the evaluation of the invasion force. Colonel Jack Hawkins responds confidently that his forces not only have the ability to accomplish the initial combat missions but also ultimately to overthrow Castro.

Bissell immediately forwards it to the president, who is said to be reassured to the point that the invasion is once again considered a go.

However, on the fourteenth, the president calls Bissell regarding the proposed air strikes that will precede the invasion. When told that as many as sixteen aircraft would be used, he tells Richard to scale it back to the eight that had been authorized. On the next day, the eight B26s carry out air strikes at dawn at three sites to destroy Cuba's air capability. Initial reports are promising, with estimates that 50 and upwards to 80 percent of Castro's air power has been destroyed on the ground at various fields. It's anticipated that the next phase of air strikes should finish the job.

When the attacks are raised at the U.N., our ambassador, Adlai Stevenson, who conspicuously has been left out of any of the briefings on what is expected to transpire, denies that the U.S. has any role in the attacks. Nonetheless, it shakes the resolve of the president and his staff. At 9:30 p.m., on the eve of the operation's launch, our people receive a telephone call from McGeorge Bundy, the president's security advisor, informing us that the additional air strikes scheduled for dawn on the day of the invasion cannot be initiated unless the invasion forces have secured a strip on their beachhead from where the planes can be launched, or at least give the appearance of being launched. This is a critical change in thinking, and Bissell, accompanied by our deputy director, General Charles P. Cabell, hustle over to the office of Dean Rusk, where the secretary of state acknowledges that on his advice, the president has taken the process one step further and has now decided to cancel the air strikes altogether.

Bissell and the general argue vehemently that the ships as well as the landings, will be seriously endangered without the strikes. Yet, when asked if they wish to speak directly with the president, both men mysteriously decline, and the order canceling the air strikes is dispatched to the departure field in Nicaragua, where the pilots are already in their cockpits, ready for takeoff.

The Joint Chiefs learn of the change of plans at varying hours in the very early morning. Warnings are forwarded to the invasion force of the likelihood, now of enemy air attacks, and the ships are instructed to expedite unloading and then withdraw from the beach.

At about 4:30 a.m., General Cabell calls Rusk at his home and renews the argument of the need to protect the ships with air cover. Finally, he makes a similar request to the president by phone but it is too late. The rest is history.

I met with Nixon last night for dinner, Dulles tells JJ over martinis.

Really, last night, Allen?

Yes, Dulles responds. By then, there was nothing to be done. By all accounts, most of the invasion forces were either dead or in the process of being rounded up and herded off to jail.

JJ nods.

I suppose, he concurs.

I told Dick it was the worst day of my life.

That might have been a little premature, Allen.

How's that, Jim?

I suspect there will be more, many more bad days before this mess blows over, Allen, many more bad days — mark my words.

Both men down their drinks in silence and signal for their bills.

JJ has just returned from a late-afternoon briefing with a Pentagon official. That's not unusual, but what he has learned is. Still, it's not until after he has started on a second neat whiskey — his beverage of choice in the office of late because it is easier to prepare than a dirty martini and is neither shaken nor stirred — that he chooses to share any of it with me. For the first few minutes, he just sits there shaking his head and muttering to himself. I have never seen him this way, even after many drinks have been consumed.

Finally, he speaks.

I can't quite figure it out. Is the president really as indecisive and incompetent as it appears, or is there something else at play here?

He stops short.

Don't you think that might be a little overstated? I muster.

I'm not so sure, he responds.

You think there's another rationale, I interject, but by this time, JJ is deep in thought and it is useless trying to prod answers out of him until he is ready to talk.

Eventually, he starts after lighting a cigarette and then quickly butting it out.

This recent mess....

The Bay of Pigs?

The slaughter of the pigs might be more appropriate.... In fact, you could make a case that the president's actions were tantamount to murder...leaving the attacking forces on the beach in such a vulnerable position.

I have never seen JJ so angry.

Our Commander-in-Chief not only called off air strikes that were intended to destroy the Cuban's capability of resisting the invasion...

Well, we know that...

...but he also, in effect, took over tactical command of the operation.

The president did?

Not directly but through his minions.

In what way?

They were deciding if and where to dispatch each ship, each warplane and telling the chairman of the Joint Chiefs of Staff what to do each step of the way.

General Lemnitzer?

Yes, Goddamn it, General Lyman L. Lemnitzer.

At one point, he was instructed to send an order to the commander in chief of the U.S. Navy forces in the Atlantic, Admiral Robert....

Dennison.

Right, an order that neither he nor the admiral understood.

How's that?

Apparently, when the admiral got the order, it was so confusing that he called General Lemnitzer on the scrambler for clarification.

Oh?

By this point, Lemnitzer is beside himself and asks Dennison where he thought the order came from. Naturally, the commander responded that he assumed it had come from the general.

That makes sense, I venture.

You would think so, JJ replies, but I am told that Lemnitzer replied, rather emphatically, that it had not, that it had come directly from 1600 Pennsylvania Avenue.

JJ lights a cigarette as he lets the magnitude of what he has just divulged set in.

So, we had all those ships sitting out there in the neutral zone waiting for something to happen but not being able to do anything, JJ continues. And, there's more.

More? I ask.

At the height of this debacle, Admiral Arleigh Burke is in a meeting with the president, imploring him to do something to rectify the situation.

Well, it was common knowledge that the military was convinced that the president would come around once the action got hot and heavy, I interject.

Maybe, but it didn't happen. At some point, after having been asked to authorize a counter-attack by the navy, JFK reiterates that he doesn't want any official U.S. involvement.

Right, I nod.

Well, Burke wasn't having any of that.

Really?

Apparently, he told him to his face: "Hell, Mr. President, we are involved."

Things must have gone downhill from there fast, I say.

Oh, yes, JJ concurs. He stops to light another cigarette from his current one before continuing.

Later in the afternoon, once it became apparent that the operation would fail, Burke made his way over to the situation room to see what could be done to minimize our losses. JJ pauses and shakes his head yet again, briefly muttering to himself.

There's no one there except one of Kennedy's military aides, Gerry McCabe, and some other junior flunky.

No one there? I ask, thinking I have misheard him.

No one of any importance. Mac Bundy and all of Kennedy's bright boys had disappeared, gone home. The admiral, McCabe, and the other fellow were left to try and pick up the pieces and coordinate whatever rescue efforts that they could.

Man, the admiral must have been pissed, I respond.

That's an understatement. Apparently, at one point, Burke just slammed down his briefcase in disgust.

JJ pauses and looks in my direction but in a manner that suggests that I'm not even there.

The admiral thinks that the whole bunch, Kennedy and his bright boys, are all God-damned cowards.

With that, JJ pulls out his attached case and starts rustling through it, looking for certain files.

I am off to the Ebbitt Hotel to talk to some of the surviving Cubans who have gathered there in the wake of the Bay of Pigs fiasco. JJ wants to hear what they have to say without them thinking that they are talking to someone who can make a difference in their situation. He doesn't say so in so many words but that's the clear impression he leaves with me.

Don't make any promises or even suggest that you are capable of doing so, he says bluntly at one point.

Just as I am about to walk out of his office, he has one last piece of advice.

When you start interviewing them, don't ask too many questions. Let them speak. Let them get their anger off their chest. Once they've done that, you'll have a bit of a roadmap to follow, and you can fine-tune your questions.

The hotel is quiet, given that mostly everyone who was involved in the operation on the ground is either dead or rotting in Cuban prisons, but eventually, I find a couple, hunkered down in a room, who had been in Nicaragua, ready to launch the air strikes.

Unsurprisingly, they are angry at everyone: Castro, the Agency, but mostly at the president.

Word has filtered down as to why the air strikes were aborted, and they cannot believe that the president had deserted them.

Of course, they have been drinking, so I am not entirely sure how much credence their ravings warrant, but they keep repeating that it is a betrayal that must be avenged.

I leave on that ominous note, having concluded that any other discussion is fruitless.

In the aftermath of the Bay of Pigs, Dulles, and to a lesser extent, the Chiefs of Staff, have given the president assurances that they will fall upon their respective swords in distancing the administration from the debacle. Still, to forestall any questions in Congress and the press, the president decides to order an inquiry in an attempt to clean up the mess before it has a chance to spread. To ensure it remains under control, he appoints Bobby to head it up along with General Maxwell Taylor, who has become the Kennedy administration's in-house military expert. Interestingly, Admiral Burke and Dulles round out the foursome, but it quickly becomes apparent that the latter two are merely window-dressing to give the appearance of a complete examination. Most notable is the handling of some of the key witnesses questioned by General Taylor and the attorney general in the absence of the CIA director and the head of the navy, despite the protestations of the admiral.

By this point, Dulles is a shadow of his former self, and despite being included in the review, it's clear that he senses that the proverbial sword of Damocles is hanging over his head. He is not alone in that regard. Richard Bissell and General Cabell are also in the administration's crosshairs as the investigation continues. Bissell, in particular, is among those interviewed by just the attorney general and General Taylor.

Aside from other perceived shortcomings, the AG has been increasingly disgruntled with Bissell ever since he learned that four members of the Alabama Air National Guard, who were in Nicaragua secretly training the Cubans, had ignored the president's orders to stand down and had flown off in their B-26s to support the invasion. The bombers had succeeded in inflicting heavy damage on the Cuban Air Force before being shot down, but no one appears to be worried much about the fate of the pilots. The biggest concern, initially, involves the possibility of them surviving and being paraded on TV by Castro in the same manner as the Russians had used Gary Powers when his U-2 reconnaissance plane had been shot down, much to the embarrassment of the Eisenhower administration.

At one point, in the presence of the president, Bissell later related to JJ that Bobby had turned to him and, poking Bissell in the chest, said: "Those American pilots had better god-damned well be dead."

It is a chilling rejoinder even for those of us who are accustomed to the expenditure of human lives while serving the greater good. Worse still, it is later learned that the administration's desire to keep its involvement under wraps extends even to denying a pension or any other financial support to the families of the four dead pilots.

We are all appalled.

A growing sense of foreboding permeates the company. The president had ordered the FBI to enter the Pentagon to determine the source of a press leak about military contingency plans to deal with the ongoing Berlin crisis, and there is increased talk that he wants to dismantle the company and replace it. But how?

Many view the events surrounding the Bay of Pigs and its aftermath as an emasculation of both the company and military by the administration. For JJ, it manifests itself in increased consumption of alcohol as well as chain smoking to the point that it appears that he only needs to light one cigarette when he first gets up each morning to keep his habit going throughout the balance of the day, which often stretches into the wee hours of the next morning. The question in some minds is what will come first: Death by cancer or immolation as a result of setting his ever-present files on fire?

I am equally worried about the amount of alcohol now being consumed daily, as evidenced by the number of late-night phone calls I am receiving. JJ is known for his prodigious work habits, but this is different. The reek of alcohol is almost discernible over the phone. His words are slurred, and his thinking is increasingly disjointed.

One weekend morning, I arrive at his office to find him slumped over his desk, snoring; his ashtray overflowing with butts. When I rouse him, he offers little explanation but sends me off on a wild-goose chase in search of some files that either never existed or have been destroyed. By the time I return, he has showered and replaced his shirt and tie, but the stench lingers throughout the remainder of the day.

Despite the president's reluctance to use the armed forces to rid himself of Castro, there is no questioning that he and Bobby will stop at nothing to achieve this objective, providing the operation remains covert.

With Bissell now in disgrace, much of the burden of trying to please them falls on Bill Harvey and Samuel Halpern — an odd couple by any definition.

Harvey is not one to mince words, and a running battle ensues with Bobby, who, in addition to his duties as the attorney general, has now become the point man on Cuba for the president. Although Harvey and the AG share certain personality characteristics, including blunt communication, they could not be more dissimilar. Harvey is hard-drinking, ill-tempered, and slovenly in appearance.

There are some among us who view Harvey with suspicion, partly because he is ex-FBI and thought to have lingering loyalties to Hoover, but also because, in every regard, he is the total antithesis of a company man. To describe his body as pear-shaped would be kind. As well, he is pigeon-toed, balding and walks around with a pistol stuffed down his pants and his shirt tail hanging out. Still, Harvey has more than proved himself in the past. Among his legendary feats is the construction of the first tunnel in Berlin, which allowed us to eavesdrop on Russian intelligence.

Both he and Halpern are in regular communication with JJ and, to a lesser extent, Richard Helms, given that Dulles is now considered a spent force and has not been seen in the office for most of the summer. If JJ knows what's up, he has been less than forthcoming.

Halpern, in particular, is shaken by how the Cuba thing is playing out.

You don't know what pressure is until you get those two SOBs laying it on you, he tells JJ. This Castro thing is like a personal vendetta.

Obsessed, Harvey adds. But the worst thing is these guys are simply amateurs. They talk a good game, but as we already know, when it comes to backing it up, forget it.

The conversation turns to the recent summit where it is reported that the president took it on the chin from Khrushchev over Cuba. That's viewed as yet another ominous development for the company since it's commonly being discussed in the administration and amongst the president's coterie that the military and the CIA let the president down.

Clearly, the president was shaken by his meeting with the Soviet leader to the point that on his return from Austria, he had to be lifted off Air Force One on a stretcher because his constantly wonky back had given out on him again.

Harvey is bemused.

What a fag, he says of the president, which is just a wee bit more respectful than his usual description of Bobby, who he refers to as the little fucker.

JJ laughs.

Are your characterizations not a little bit influenced by your first meeting with the president, Bill?

Huh? Harvey grunts.

I hear the president asked to meet you, JJ continues, because he had been told you are the company's equivalent of James Bond.

Harvey scowls as JJ guffaws at the absurdity of the rotund agent being cast in the manner of 007.

What did he say to you, Bill?

Harvey just shakes his head in anger.

Asked you, didn't he, whether you've had as much success with the ladies as James Bond?

For Christ's sake, Harvey explodes. What do you expect from some asshole who is so deluded as to think that a paperback fantasy character is representative of real agents like ourselves?

Well, the president fancies himself a ladies' man, JJ continues.

At this point, Halpern decides to add to the fun.

You know, Bill, his dick is hanging out of his pants more often than that shirttail of yours.

JJ is convulsed in laughter as Harvey storms out of his office. But it's a rare moment of levity in otherwise increasingly difficult times.

It's official. They're out.

No one had talked much about it during the summer, even though the extended absences of Dulles, Bissell, and General Cabell could not be ignored.

But now we know.

It's hard to imagine an American Secret Service without the man from upstate New York: Allen Welsh Dulles. He has been involved here in some shape or form dating back to the Thirties when he served as the station chief in Berne, Switzerland, for the Office of Strategic Services, the precursor to the OAS and eventually the company.

Office lore has it that early in his career in Switzerland, Allen was on duty one weekend day when he received an urgent phone call from a certain Vladimir Ilyich Ulyanov, better known as Vladimir Lenin, asking to meet with him. Apparently, Dulles had scheduled a tennis match that afternoon with a comely lass and turned him down. The next day, as the story goes, Lenin was deported on a sealed train to St. Petersburg, Russia.

Later, Dulles was a major player in Operation Sunrise, the secret and controversial negotiations at the end of the war that resulted in the surrender of German forces in northern Italy.

I'm told that at one point, he was meeting face-to-face with a Waffen-SS general, Karl Wolff, in Lucerne. When I mention it to JJ, he chuckles softly.

You know who else was involved? He asks, then answers before I can reply: General Lyman Lemnitzer.

My surprise at hearing the name of the recently deposed head of the Joint Chiefs of Staff provokes yet another smile.

The Russians were not amused when they learned that their two so-called allies in the war against fascism — the British and ourselves, were conducting negotiations behind their backs with the enemy, JJ continues.

How did they find out? I ask.

Oh, it had to come from the British side, although it's never been proven, JJ responds. More than a few scenarios point to my old friend Kim Philby as the culprit.

A cloud passes over his face at the mention of his former British friend and colleague.

But Philby's still in their service, is he not? I ask.

Beirut, working undercover as a correspondent for the *London Times*, JJ responds.

I suppose that's safe ground for the minute, he continues, although who knows when it comes to the Middle East. The Soviets are very anxious to build on their current ties with Nasser and the Egyptians.

Then, the reminiscences turn back to Dulles and his storied career.

JJ relates how Dulles, through his contacts, was aware of

the plot to assassinate Hitler but was told by his superiors not to get involved, even though a successful coup would have shortened the war.

His involvement as an advisor to Dewey's campaign set his career back momentarily when Truman surprised one and all by upsetting the New York Governor in the 1948 election. However, with a Republican administration in play in 1953, Eisenhower made him the first civilian to head up our agency.

In total, Dulles had served about 30 years in the company through its various incarnations and, in the process, under four presidents, three of them of a different political stripe. It's hard to know whether it's simply his politics that's finally caught up with him or whether other elements are in play here.

For a week or so, JJ is in a real funk, hiding out in his suite, immersed in his files, reflective of the dispirited nature that prevails throughout the campus.

Finally, he emerges from his self-imposed isolation to announce the holding of a party. Nothing quite like those Fifties' bashes where liaisons of many natures flourished. This one's strictly in-house in the wake of Dulles being sacked along with Bissell and General Cabell.

In addition to the guests of honor, many of the key players attend along with their wives or other interests. To name a few, they include Richard Helms, Samuel Halpern, Bill Harvey, Desmond FitzGerald, Miles Copeland, Cord Meyer Jr., and Frank Gardiner Wisner, our man in London, who some think has returned home for more shock therapy to combat his increasing bouts of manic depression.

There is much drinking. Cord, who has become

increasingly combative since splitting with his wife Mary, confronts Frank, who at one time was his best friend in the company as well as his superior. With smoke curling in and around the one eye he lost in World War 2, 'The Cyclops,' as he is known, pokes his finger in Wisner's chest and declares:

"You're a shell of the man you once were."

Several people, Harvey in particular, are prepared to take it up outside with Meyer, but Wisner waves them off, putting his arm around his former protege and leading him to a corner.

There, they are overheard in an animated discussion regarding the president and his brother, as it's well-known that Cord has a love-hate relationship with JFK, having been neighbors with the president in Hickory Hill in the Fifties. Later, when Bobby and his clan took over the home and the grounds, the relationship expanded.

In fact, company folklore has it that at one party, Cord suggested that everyone jump in the pool naked. Ethel probably made the plunge; not sure about Bobby.

Now, however, the talk revolves around the ongoing relationship between Cord's ex, Mary, and the president, which Cord, like all of us, is hearing more about and liking less despite his and Mary's permanent estrangement.

In fact, before the sacking of Dulles, Allen and JJ had discussed transcripts of tapes made of Mary talking on the phone to the president. And there are other sources of information that JJ is jealously guarding, which are equally explosive in nature.

After midnight, however, the uninhibited consumption of alcohol begins to take effect, and talk is replaced by dancing and other various flirtations. At one point, JJ is seen standing in the corner dancing — or should I say gyrating — by himself to an Elvis Presley tune. Everyone is amused.

By dawn, only a few of us remain, including Dulles. Exhaustion aside, the talk turns to JJ's files. Dulles, in particular, wants to know what's turned up.

JJ gets right to the point, noting that despite our president's sore back after the Austrian fiasco with Khrushchev, it hasn't constrained his sexual appetite.

Mmmm, Dulles murmurs knowingly.

It's been party time all summer in the White House, JJ continues.

Dulles smiles. Just like old times in Washington, he allows, when all the wives would decamp to Maryland or Virginia leaving the boys at loose ends with all those lovely young belles in the secretarial pool.

That's right, Allen, and in this case, the first lady has been absent on a regular basis. In fact, the president only sees her on weekends at the compound in Hyannis Port. On the few occasions she's been in the area, she's more than likely at their farm in Virginia.

And the president's companions? Dulles inquires.

Too numerous to mention, Allen, JJ responds.

The principals, however, are Fiddle and Faddle, as they are commonly known.

Fiddle and Faddle? Dulles queries.

Two secretaries in the White House, Jill Cowen and Patricia Weir, JJ explains.

They are regulars at the pool parties that take place during the lunch hours at the White House.

Pool parties? Dulles raises a puzzled eyebrow.

Right, everybody jumps in naked and…. I don't need to

explain any further. Do I, Allen?

I suppose not, Dulles concurs.

Both men sink back into their chairs, and for a moment, I think they've fallen asleep.

But Dulles isn't finished.

What else, he inquires?

Mary Meyer often enjoys dinner and other pleasures with the president. Dave Powers often signs in as Powers plus one. But you know that.

Yes, we've gone over that ground before, Dulles responds brusquely.

At that point, JJ snaps to attention, having forgotten something.

You know, it's more than just screwing around, he says.

The president actually has his Secret Service agents running up photos of himself and his female friends in various stages of undress to the Mickelson Gallery, here in Washington, for framing.

What? Dulles exclaims.

Oh, yea, JJ continues. They bring the pictures into the gallery in the morning, and the proprietor takes measurements. Then, the agents leave with the pics in their possession.

Sometimes, the president and his friends have masks on — I don't know what that's all about — but there's no questioning that the president is one of the people in the photos.

My, my, Dulles murmurs.

Right, so when the agents return that evening and the proprietor puts the pictures in the newly created frames. . . .

Matted as well, I suppose? Dulles interjects.

I guess so, JJ allows. I'm not an expert on framing. . . . I'm only interested in the photos.

It's pretty brazen, Jim, this whole business, Dulles muses.

I can't imagine someone in his position being so reckless, JJ says. I mean, all these liaisons are already bad enough, but to actually allow the creation of a trail of evidence. It's beyond my comprehension.

It's almost as if he's trying to distract us, Allen.

Dulles just shakes his head.

Oh, no, well, I, ah…what do you mean, Jim?

I'm not quite sure yet, JJ responds, looking equally tired and confused.

Time for me to go, Dulles says, pushing himself awkwardly out of the chair.

Keep me informed.

JJ nods in agreement.

I'm not sure if we should be surprised that the president is backing off confronting the Russians, JJ allows in a rare moment of introspection.

How's that? I ask.

It's in his blood.

Old Joe Kennedy did his best to keep America out of the Second World War. In fact, you could argue that he seemed more determined to support the Nazis than defeat them.

By the way, General LeMay's of the same opinion.

I have to laugh.

What's so funny, JJ asks.

Well, from what I hear, General LeMay only has one

position…

And that is? JJ interjects.

…that we should bomb the hell out of the Russkies and anyone who supports them.

JJ laughs as well.

I suppose that's correct, he lets out.

It's a rare moment when we both can laugh at the situation, but it doesn't last long as JJ picks back up on his concerns.

This wall the Russians are putting up in Berlin is very serious, and we haven't made any attempt to counter it.

But what can we do? I wonder aloud. It's not as if we can mobilize extra units and confront the Russian construction teams. The wall is well inside their area of control. Effectively, our forces in Berlin are surrounded by them, so it would be particularly difficult to reinforce them, much less support them in any realistic way.

Our man in Berlin, David Murphy, has an interesting view, JJ responds.

He says the message that the president has consistently conveyed to the Soviets is that they have the right to control their own sector….

There's silence as we both mull that over. JJ is slumped in his chair, dragging on yet another cigarette. Suddenly, he sits up straight.

It's not just the president that has sent that signal, he adds.

He grabs a folder with some press clippings from the back of a metal file holder on his desk. He leafs through the various clippings until he comes to one that has an area marked on each side of the text.

Here it is, he exclaims and passes it to me.

The story deals with a television interview with Arkansas Senator William Fulbright, who is chairman of the Senate Foreign Relations Committee.

"I don't understand why the East Germans don't close their border," the story quotes Fulbright, "because I think they have the right to close it."

So, it's not just the president, I note.

Read the notation from Murphy at the bottom of the clipping, JJ instructs.

I look at a scrawl in red ink. That statement, it reads, could not have been made without advance presidential approval. It is understood here that the president never had any intention of challenging the erection of The Wall.

So, it was a fait accompli, JJ interjects, and the Soviets probably knew that before they put up the first partition, thanks to the president's back-channel communications with Bolshakov or whatever Russian the president has been carrying out secret communications with.

Well, I respond, I don't know if we can conclude that the president was complicit in any way. Now that I think of it, even Bill Harvey agrees with the president on this one, and you know how much he loves our commander-in-chief.

JJ scowls. It's a defeatist mentality, just the same as after the Second World War when we didn't want to antagonize the Russians, and we let them get away with murder.

Murder? I ask.

Oh, for Christ's sake, JJ responds. You know very well what I mean. We let them solidify their hold on all of those Eastern European countries without hardly a murmur of opposition.

I suppose we didn't want any more confrontations, I respond lamely.

Yea, he agrees, slumping back into his chair and raising his mug. We were sick of war, sick of the killing....

That's right.

Except, he says, sitting up straight again and pounding his hand on his desk. We had just fought a bloody long, and costly battle against tyranny and repression with the Nazis, only to allow another form of fascism to fill the vacuum.

There's not much I can muster in response, and JJ returns to a mound of files on the corner of his desk, dismissing me, yet again without any further word.

I have just returned from spending several weeks in what seemed to me like Hell.

Everyone was envious when they heard my itinerary — Seattle, Palm Springs, Hollywood, and then Hawaii — and under most circumstances, they are great places to visit, but these are not ordinary times.

I am barely back in the office, having taken a red-eye from L.A. when JJ is ready for a debriefing.

Without even the faintest attempt at small talk, he unloads a barrage of questions.

You met with the sheriff in Seattle? He confirmed what we had learned from Larry Newman? His 'baptism of fire?'

I had never seen JJ so impatient and intense, animated almost to the point of a frenzy, lighting one cigarette from another before the first one was half-finished.

Larry Newman had joined the Secret Service in 1960 and

was quickly promoted to the presidential detail in the fall of 1961. What he experienced and observed on the West Coast with the president had shaken him severely.

The president was to speak in Seattle and Newman, and Clint Hill, a senior agent, had flown there in advance to arrange for security at the Olympic Hotel where the president and his entourage would be staying. Everything went according to the plan initially, and when the president arrived at the hotel, the floor he was staying on was sealed.

Newman said he and Hill were stationed in front of the presidential suite on the night in question when they heard a commotion by the elevator. Naturally, they were concerned, and their apprehension was further heightened when a party of several policemen and firemen came around the corner, as well as two women and another man who quickly identified himself as the local sheriff.

Newman had told us that it was evident from Hill's reaction that he had been through something like this before. It was also apparent that the sheriff and the policemen were very familiar with the ladies in question. Obviously, they were hookers, possibly what might pass in Seattle for 'high-class girls,' and the sheriff was intent on delivering them personally to the president.

Hill stepped forward to stop them, which raised even more of a ruckus, bringing out Dave Powers, a top presidential aide, Newman told us. When Powers started to escort the ladies into the presidential suite, the sheriff was very disturbed that he was being deprived of delivering his goods first-hand. However, Powers was having nothing of that, and eventually, the sheriff was reduced to bidding his charges goodbye, but not before he issued a warning that if anything ever came up about that night, he would make sure that the girls ended up in Stillicoom, which Newman later learned was a state psych institution.

As disgusted as he was with what had transpired, Newman was equally embarrassed that he was unprepared for this type of activity. When one of the policemen accompanying the sheriff asked whether it happened all of the time, Newman said he didn't know what to say.

All of the rooms on the floor were booked for the president's traveling party, which was considerable, and in addition to JFK's suite, both Kenny O'Donnell and Powers had suites at the end of the hall.

Much later that evening, Newman told us, he had made what he thought would be a routine security check along the corridors of the U-shaped hotel and found six unmanned fire exits, which were supposed to be guarded by Seattle policemen. Moments later, he discovered a group of them in a fire escape, watching O'Donnell in a three-way with the two girls, who apparently had already finished servicing the president.

It seems that O'Donnell had neglected to pull the blinds in his room, and the policemen were passing a pair of binoculars back and forth amongst themselves. The sergeant in charge quickly apologized, and the men returned to their stations. However, by this point, Newman was extremely disturbed by the breakdown in security that he had witnessed.

Later when he talked with Hill about it, the senior agent told him it was common practice when the president was on the road that hookers would be brought in for him and some of the senior staff accompanying him. Usually, Hill told him, Powers would round up a few locals and just breeze through security with little more than a: "How are you, pal," to the men responsible for protecting the president. Efforts to stop the practice were quickly rebuked by the president's senior staff. Hill was apologetic, Newman said, acknowledging that the Secret Service never knew whether the president would be dead or alive when the next morning dawned. Morale was extremely low, and it was then that it dawned on Newman why he had been able to get what seemed like a plumb assignment so early in his career.

My job in Seattle was to see if I could contact the 'Ladies of the Night' to further confirm what Newman told us, but my efforts went for naught. Although the sheriff involved initially confirmed what had happened, he quickly turned hostile when I suggested meeting with the ladies. After a couple of days of nosing around with little success, I headed for Palm Springs to talk to some local state troopers.

JJ had heard about a party there at Bing Crosby's that had gotten particularly out of hand.

Apparently, the troopers had been assigned to road duty on the perimeter of the estate, but there was so much noise coming from the house that they decided maybe they should investigate.

So, you looked up the guys I told you about, and…? JJ enquired.

They were a little reluctant to talk at first, I told him, but then they loosened up after a few beers.

Okay, and…

It was quite a party. Peter Lawford was there. Crosby. Some starlets and a bunch of airline stewardesses.

How nice, JJ allows.

Not Lawford, I continued.

Oh?

Apparently, the troopers had to rescue some young thing from his clutches out in the desert.

JJ just shakes his head.

He was falling over drunk, determined to share an intimate moment with the young lady, and had chased her out into the cactus.

JJ starts to laugh.

Well, in her mind, I guess, it was not in the script, at least not with Lawford.

Who knows? I countered. But they left him lying in the desert, passed out.

What else? JJ asked.

Apparently, it was just like the White House lunch parties. Everyone was carrying on around the pool…

Naked?

Of course.

And the state troopers?

They didn't know what to do, so they just hung around on the periphery to keep an eye on things.

The president was having fun?

You better believe it. But not as much fun as Dave Powers.

Oh…

At one point, Powers was banging some broad on the diving board…

What?

…much to the president's amusement.

Okay, so?

I'm guessing Powers was pretty drunk…

Right.

Anyway, after finishing with the woman, he goes into Crosby's house and comes out after a short while wearing a suit.

JJ looks puzzled.

Powers was dressed in one of Bing Crosby's suits?

That's right, I continue, sans shirt, shoes, socks and tie.

Just the suit?

Right. So he jumps onto the diving board and…

I start to laugh.

And?

He does a huge belly flop in the pool.

With the suit on?

Yes, with the suit on.

Oh, really, JJ says, shaking his head in amazement.

Well, I continue, the president thinks it's hilarious.

I guess he does, JJ chuckles.

So, Powers goes back into the house and puts on another fancy suit.

Now JJ can barely contain himself. What is Crosby doing?

Apparently, he didn't object too much to the first suit going in the pool, at least not to the point of appearing angry.

But the second…?

The troopers say he's getting steamed.

But that doesn't stop Powers from diving into the pool?

Oh, no, in fact, he goes back for yet another.

JJ just shakes his head.

A third suit?

So, I ask JJ, these guys, top officials, they're nothing more than clowns. Are they just crazy, or what?

JJ stares at me long and hard before answering. His increasingly tight, gaunt cheeks, almost imperceptibly, twitching.

Sycophants. Plain and simple.

They'll do anything to get his attention and amuse him.

And it's not just his flunkies.

Oh?

One of my Harvard sources, JJ continues, overheard a conversation with a Henry Kissinger, who had been in Washington recently and met with the president.

Kissinger? I haven't heard of him.

Apparently, he's some German-born professor who is serving as a consultant on European affairs for the National Security Council.

Okay.

So, he's invited to a Cabinet Room meeting during the crisis in Berlin, you know, after the Austria debacle.

I nod my head.

Anyway, JJ continues, he's at the cabinet meeting, and everyone's seated around the table when the president comes in.

JJ pauses for what seems like a minute as if he's remembered something that should be included. Then he's back in the present again.

Where was I?

Cabinet meeting.

Right. So, everyone stands up when the president comes in.

They're supposed to.

JJ shakes his head, more in amazement than disagreement.

Yes, they are, he continues.

Then, a White House steward comes in with a tureen of soup.

Clam chowder?

Even in summer.

JJ pauses yet again.

So, Kissinger says the steward serves the soup and crackers to the president and Bobby and then leaves.

No one else gets served?

That's right. It's as if the president and his brother think they are some kind of royalty....

They have a sense of entitlement, I venture.

Something like that, he responds.

There's a silence between us as JJ shuffles some files and lights another cigarette.

The smoke is really starting to get to me. I cough and pretend to clear my throat, but to no avail.

Finally, he looks up.

Hawaii?

I check my notes before answering.

Ah, I talked to a Marine Colonel out there who kinda confirms what we've been told.

From Newman?

Right.

About Kennedy using Admiral Felt's residence to screw yet some more hookers?

Well, initially, the Colonel thought they were secretaries, I respond.

Secretaries?

Yea, apparently, that's what he was told when these, ah, ladies showed up.

JJ considers this morsel of information for a moment.

And, then?

Well, I answer, the fact that I'm out there snooping around has probably raised some suspicions.

That's not our problem, JJ responds.

It could be, I answer, if the president gets wind of it.

JJ contemplates that possibility for the moment and then appears to dismiss it.

I can't be concerned about that, he responds.

Alright, I agree.

So, anyway, JJ says, the president is staying at the residence of the commander of the Pacific Fleet…

Harry Felt, I confirm.

Yea, Commander Felt and….

Well, they bring in drinks and food that the president likes, and then these two ladies, who are not on any guest list, suddenly show up.

And? JJ persists.

Well, it makes for a very awkward situation, to say the least.

You know, it's not just the Colonel now who knows about them.

There's all the staff at the commander's residence. A bunch of other people….

You're right, says JJ excitedly. There's a lot of people talking about the president's behavior. Eventually, it's got to come back to bite him…and it won't necessarily be tied to us.

I suppose, I start to agree.

But it doesn't look good for us to be out there, or in Seattle, asking all of these questions about the president's behavior.

We're not alone, JJ responds.

How's that? I ask.

If we're hearing about it, so's Hoover. You can count on that.

I shrug. I suppose so.

JJ's not done yet.

LA? It's Marilyn, right?

Yes, I concede, it's Miss Monroe.

You make it sound like we're discussing a saint?

No, she's definitely no saint, I say resignedly.

So, what do we know? JJ asks.

It sounds like some sort of menage-a-trois.

A threesome?

Not at the same time, but if I understand it correctly, both the president and Bobby are infatuated with Marilyn, and it doesn't stop there.

So, let's get to the details, JJ presses.

Well, I guess Peter Lawford and his wife….

Patricia, the president's sister.

Right, they introduced him to Marilyn…even before the election.

Okay.

So, apparently, he uses their home in Santa Monica for his assignations with Miss Monroe when he's in L.A.

Really? Are they there at the time?

I don't know.

C'mon, give me something, JJ implores.

There's kind of a love-hate relationship here between Marilyn and the president and his brother.

Oh, really, JJ responds, signaling impatiently to me with a hand to continue.

Well, I guess one moment, she loves both of them deeply and is declaring to one and all that she will never do anything to hurt the president or his brother.

Uh-huh.

And the next thing, when she's depressed.... Well, that's a different matter.

How's that?

Apparently, she's on all kinds of medication.

Like the president, JJ says with a smirk, which I ignore.

Well, when she's off the drugs, she gets depressed, starts saying all kinds of things, and the president has to send out people, like his long-time friend, ah, Charles...

... Spalding, JJ interjects.

Yes, apparently, JFK sent him out during the election to get Marilyn under control.

Hospitalized?

Something like that.

And, I suppose, JJ says, Peter Lawford helped Spalding do that?

Right.

Part of the reason she gets depressed, I add, is that she knows she's simply being used.

Of course, she's being used.

No, I insist, not in that way.

What do you mean, JJ responds.

She knows that he's also doing other starlets when he's out there and even back in Washington.

Oh, really?

Yea, Angie Dickenson and Gene Tierney are the two most prominent. Dean Martin and Sinatra helped set him up with them and others.

JJ seems lost momentarily as he contemplates this new intelligence.

And, one more thing.

JJ looks up. More?

A couple of the president's sisters, who travel with him, are trying to screw some of the Secret Service guys. It's a really bad scene. One of them's very aggressive. They call her 'Rancid Ass.'

Sounds delightful, JJ responds. What a family.

By the way, I add, these are just some of the things that the Secret Service knows about.

JJ looks at me intently, his curiosity clearly piqued.

Apparently, I continue, the president has been playing games with them.

Games?

He likes to try and lose them on occasion.

JJ continues to stare intently at me. Tiny beads of sweat appear on his forehead.

Explain, he demands.

They think it involves women. Trying to hide some of his liaisons from them.

But that makes no sense, JJ counters. He's very open about his relationships with women. In fact, as Allen pointed out, he is recklessly bold....

They think he just wants to play games with them. Messing with their heads like he does with others.

And you? JJ asks.

They're probably right, I allow after some contemplation.

But what if they aren't? JJ counters.

I wouldn't want to go down that path. I nervously respond as I edge towards the door.

You might not, but.... JJ begins and then abruptly stops, apparently transfixed by the unthinkable.

John McCone is our new boss, having replaced Allen, and it is upsetting JJ more than even I had anticipated. But it's not just that JJ had developed a secure relationship with Dulles over the years. McCone is seen as being from outside the culture and is viewed as just another way in which the president is asserting more power over the agency, possibly even taking it over.

So, what's the deal with McCone? I ask JJ.

He shakes his head resignedly.

He's a businessman who's convinced himself that he knows what it takes to run the country's top national security agency.

Based on his experience as chairman of the U.S. Atomic Energy Commission?

Exactly!

Well.... I start.

He's a God-damned amateur, JJ explodes.

Oh, I respond, startled by JJ's rare show of temper.

He's the guy who leaked the file about Israel building the Dimona nuclear plant in the Negev Desert to the *New York Times*, for Christ's sake. It was a secret and a key element in Israel's national security….

I hadn't heard that, but I suppose it makes it more difficult for our allies, I note, reflecting on the fact that JJ has many connections to the Israeli Secret Service and is, in fact, considered our principal liaison with the Mossad.

Yea, well, the president is fixated on nuclear weapons, and…. JJ continues but then suddenly changes course.

I don't know what to think other than that Richard Helms is making moves that suggest….

He stops without finishing the thought, then continues.

You watch Helms; he's going to play McCone. He wants to run this place, and he's not going to let a little thing like a presidential appointment change his plans.

You like Helms…?

JJ pauses.

We've been through a lot together, but something about him makes me nervous.

Oh?

I don't trust men who pretend to be drinkers but are not.

Pretend?

Yea, Helms has one martini and calls it a night.

So?

I guess he doesn't trust himself to have more than one.

I can't help but laugh, knowing JJ's penchant for martinis,

wine, and, of late, bourbon.

So, he doesn't drink much, I venture. I guess that's out of character with most of us, but…

I don't know what he does outside of here, aside from playing tennis, JJ says, but it appears to me that he's rather adept at plying us with drinks in order to develop false confidences.

Oh?

Helms is ambitious….

The thought drifts off into thin air as JJ re-immerses himself in his papers.

JJ is in an expansive mood, having just returned from one of his customary lengthy lunches at the Rive Gauche in Georgetown, where cocktails lead to red wine and, inevitably, cognac with disturbing results.

His guest today was Cord Meyers, a regular in that regard and a well-known favorite of JJ, having embraced with great enthusiasm my mentor's phobia about communism.

Despite their differences in age, Meyer and JJ share several traits, including a predilection for the bohemian lifestyle and poetry. In fact, I wasn't surprised to learn that JJ had edited a literary journal at Yale, *Furioso*, that published the works of e. e. cummings and Ezra Pound, among others.

The war had not been easy for Cord, having first lost his twin brother and then later his left eye when a grenade exploded in his face in a foxhole in Guam. Upon his return, he turned to writing and working for peace. In 1946, his short story, *Waves of Darkness*, based on his war experiences, captured the O. Henry Prize for the first published story. In those early post-war years, he dedicated himself to honoring those "who fell beside me" by attempting to make the world a better place through his efforts as president of the United World Federalists, an organization dedicated to the naïve concept of developing a world government. Apparently, he not only wowed all the girls in the colleges he visited but it's said that his boyish good looks, contrasted by the disfigurement of his left eye, made for a compelling peace poster that adorned many a college girl's wall.

Back then, the Jaycees, for one, picked him as one of America's ten most outstanding young men, along with an up-and-coming California congressman, Richard Nixon.

But then he changed, although it would be some time before it became public. It's hard to get a read on Cord, even at the best of times. Maybe he simply grew up, or his role with the United World Federalists was part of an exercise designed to create a cover for him so that he could move freely among various groups without arousing suspicions. Regardless, Meyer became part of a wave of idealistic, anti-communist liberals recruited by us to counteract the communist menace that allegedly was infiltrating labor unions, youth groups, and other organizations predisposed to changing the world. Still, in some people's eyes, it wasn't always clear in the early Fifties as to whose side Cord was on.

At one point, he became a target for Senator Joseph McCarthy's witch hunt, based on his earlier experiences with the United World Federalists. Like many, he was left to dangle for a time until Allen and Richard Helms came to his rescue. Still, it was JJ's influence that prevailed after his supposed rehabilitation, and from it emerged a deep and abiding distrust for communism and anything associated with it.

For weeks, JJ has been laying low, or so I think. Out of the office? Never. On holidays? Not that he ever takes holidays.

And then, suddenly, Langley is abuzz with excitement. Apparently, we've landed a whopper from the Soviets. Anatoly Golitsyn. And JJ has been debriefing him.

I arrive the next day to find him holed up in his vault suite, poring over files.

So, we've hooked a big one. Congratulations.

JJ smiles warily. He takes off his glasses to clean the already huge lens that seems to be getting bigger each time I see him.

It's not good, he finally admits.

Golitsyn?

No, no. What I've discovered through our interrogation.

I wait for him patiently to continue.

Had to fend off Helms first.

Why would Helms think he should have control of a defector? You're chief of counterintelligence.

Precisely, but Richard wants to be in charge.

Still, McCone backed you?

More or less, I suppose, he answers.

JJ looks even more gaunt than in the past if that is possible. His sunken cheeks, contrasted by burning eyes, give the appearance of an El Greco painting.

That damn Philby, he says at last. I knew I should have pushed the file harder against him…

Philby, huh?

…Ten years ago or so, when Maclean and Burgess made a

run for it.

Who? I ask.

Donald Maclean and Guy Burgess. They both defected to the Soviet Union.

From us?

No, no, they're Brits, he says, shaking his head incredulously. Maclean was in the foreign office, high up, second secretary. Burgess was here in Washington....

JJ starts to laugh.

He was living with Kim, for Chris-sakes, in a house on Nebraska Avenue. Both of them were intelligence officers masquerading as diplomats. You know how it works.

I nod in agreement.

So, JJ continues, you know about the Verona file?

My blank face suggests otherwise.

It was information we were gathering on Soviet infiltration of the British Secret Service.

Oh, really, I respond in an effort to keep him talking.

Anyway, Philby had access to it, and we cleared it several years earlier.

By you? I ask.

JJ puts down his glasses in disgust.

Let's not go there!

My body language signals acquiescence, and JJ resumes his narrative.

I always thought that Philby had tipped off the pair of them, but the Brits wouldn't listen. Even though Bedell....

General Bedell Smith? I interject. One of our former directors?

Our director at the time. In no uncertain terms, he gave the Brits an ultimatum, I suppose, that Philby had to be canned, or we were breaking off our joint intelligence relationship.

Again, he pauses.

I suppose that's not entirely true….

What's not entirely true? I ask.

Ah, that the Brits didn't listen. They forced Philby to resign and grilled him for over a year. Everybody was convinced that he was the third man, the Russian mole we all had suspected but could never prove.

And? I ask.

He never broke. It's amazing. So, they eventually reinstated him, he snorts with derision. In fact, Harold Mcmillan….

The British Prime Minister?

He was the foreign secretary at that time. He said he was clean or something to that effect.

So, I interject, Golitsyn is confirming your suspicions about Philby?

JJ lights a cigarette and his eyes wander off into the far reaches of the vault.

Much more than that, he murmurs. Much, much more.

He waves me out.

I'll talk to you later.

Again, days have passed, and no sign of JJ.

Rumors abound in the corridors and in the deepest recesses of the senior suites, albeit nothing concrete.

Then, late at night, the phone rings

It's JJ, and he's been drinking.

He starts reciting some poetry.

I suspect it's T.S. Eliot from *Gerontion* since it is his favorite.

One stanza, in particular, has a dark side to it:

After such knowledge, what forgiveness? Think now

JJ intones in a raspy, gravelly voice.

History has many cunning passages, contrived corridors

And issues, deceives with whispering ambitions,

Guides us by vanities

There is silence, so I ask him what it all means, but his answer is even more confusing.

It's as if, he says, we're in a wilderness of mirrors.

A what? I ask, thinking I have misheard him because I am still groggy from being awakened at such a time.

The KGB, he continues, is capable of manipulating us to believe what it desires, and we, we can't…we are neither capable of identifying nor defending ourselves from this…this manipulation.

Like what, I ask?

You know, where defectors are false, lies are truth, truth lies, and the reflections leave you dazed and confused. He carries on for much longer, with most of it becoming increasingly incoherent. I am starting to worry about the country's future and wondering about the role that the Kingfisher and other like-minded souls will play in determining it.

1962

Truth is always complicated
when it comes to defectors...and traitors.

The new year is ushered in with a blast of wintry weather, but in the Virginia farmhouse compound just outside of Washington, where Anotoliy Mikhalovich Golitsyn is being safeguarded and debriefed, the temperature is rising with each revelation painstakingly wormed out of an otherwise somewhat recalcitrant defector — or at least that is the impression being left with his handlers. For one thing, the guest of honor refuses to talk, except in the presence of only the most senior people, hence JJ's involvement. It's said that his initial demands included being debriefed by McCone, which most thought to be hilarious, given that the director is essentially a bureaucrat with no real experience in the intelligence field. Also, Golitsyn seems to think he is worthy of meeting with the president. I don't know what left people rolling their eyes more — the thought of a defector meeting with the president or being debriefed by McCone. Golitsyn's apparent lack of reality has got some people questioning his bona fides, but not JJ, who senses a kindred spirit in this Russian enigma, particularly when it comes to drinking, for which he and Anotoliy share a certain fondness.

To further complicate matters, we are completing a major move from our previously cramped offices in the 'L' Building in West Potomac Park, Washington, to what many consider will be Dulles' legacy, a capacious new complex at Langley. Sadly, Allen is not part of the working environment of what he often referred to, in the planning stages, as the campus.

It is hard to describe the entire structure adequately, so I will limit my observations to the new premises for our group. We are located on the southwest corner of the second floor, taking up most of the two corridors of the building's center and side wings. Our rooms, like the corridors, are painted institution gray. The outer office consists of a large reception room with a sofa, chairs, some magazines, and three secretaries. JJ's long-time personal assistant of German extraction, Bertha Dasenburg, serves as the gatekeeper. She has been officially on staff since 1952, when JJ was named Director of Counterintelligence, but has links dating back to Italy where, ostensibly, she was connected with the Red Cross during the Second World War. There are whispers that she was involved with JJ's underground activities at the time. Regardless of her past, there is no doubt that Bertha now has the authority to grant or deny access to the boss — a power that she wields with Nazi-like authority and considerable efficiency. Woe to anyone who dares to cross her.

The inner office, at 20 to 25 feet, is reasonably large but not overwhelming by institutional standards. The windows on the far wall are covered with Venetian blinds that are opened each morning by Bertha but then closed as soon as JJ arrives. It is a curious dynamic in which neither party challenges the other overtly. The most important part of her daily routine involves removing the active files from the various black safes in the walls of the outer office and placing them on JJ's desk so that they are ready and available for his perusal when he arrives around mid-morning each day. The volume of the files — constantly expanding — threatens to overwhelm even his king-sized wooden desk as well as the two adjoining side tables.

At times, the stack is so high it makes JJ invisible, even when seated in his high-back, leather chair behind a desk, which would otherwise dominate any room. Significantly, the desk is situated in such a way as to ensure that no one can stand behind JJ. Often, the only clue that JJ is present is the constant curling plume of smoke, which only adds to the gloom of a room without light due to the shuttered blinds. For the most part, the only source of illumination is a small desk lamp and it, too, is overwhelmed by the mounds of files, the smoke and the lack of outside light.

Aside from the many safes dotting the walls of the outer office, the piece de resistance is the special vault room built to JJ's specifications across the hall. In theory, access to this secure chamber is granted only in the presence of JJ or Bertha, but I overheard Bertha complaining to the other secretaries that the boss still has not provided her with the access code and that she questions whether he will do so. How will anyone gain access if something happens to him, she wonders? The vault has specially strengthened walls, an electronic pushbutton entry system for access during working hours, and a combination door lock for night security. It is the heart of JJ's secret world.

Some outsiders might question why we need so much safe capacity, but already the exterior safes are full to brimming, and the vault seems to be equally well stocked with files. This is due in no small part to JJ's compulsion for controlling as much material as possible. Nothing is ever shredded and despite some of the advances made with computers of late, none are in our employ.

Essentially, JJ refuses to allow any of his precious secrets or even the most basic minutiae to make its way out of our office and into the mainstream of the Company. As a result, we are constantly at war with the Soviet Bloc Division staff, who have taken up residence on the fourth and fifth floors and are actually running operations around the world and behind the Iron Curtain. The Soviet bloc staff is increasingly resentful of JJ's methods and personal style. Several are emigrés from eastern Europe or, at best, first-generation Americans; all imbued with a passionate hatred of Stalinism and all things communist. They worry that some of their operations may be at risk because of the barriers that JJ has thrown up in his efforts to maintain total control over each and every shred of information that comes our way.

The trouble with Jim, these operational agents mutter over coffee and cigarettes in the corridors, and vodka or slivovitz and cigars in the dark recesses of their offices, is that he has never broken an agent or — even more damning — caught a spy. To make matters worse, they point out that not a single member of JJ's staff can properly interrogate defectors because none speak Russian. How, they wonder, can JJ adequately assess the information he is obtaining from Golitsyn if he is incapable of understanding the nuances of what this new prize has to tell us because all of the conversations are in English: Golitsyn's second or third language?

Ironically, if they only knew how little useful intel relating to modern KGB and GRU operations is contained in all of the safes with their burgeoning troves of papers and documents, their hostilities would be lessened, but then again, our role in the larger scheme of things would be extremely diminished, if not eliminated.

Those of us in JJ's shadow are considered to be fundamentalists, people for whom counterintelligence is not merely a job but a calling. We are not action people, myself to a limited degree excluded, but rather, movers of paper, committed to seeking coherent patterns from the contradictions and confusion that is counterintelligence. In return for our loyalty, disciples receive his patronage and professional support, which was considerable during Dulles' tenure. Because of our lack of working assets, all of the staff are reduced to reinvestigating the past for any scraps of information that had not been fully analyzed. Not surprisingly, revisionism runs rampant.

Our lead investigator is Raymond Rocca, the second of JJ's two major assistants. The other is Clare Edward Petty, who heads up the Special Investigation Group. Raymond acts as head of our new Research and Analysis Department and is well-suited for the task as he has an excellent memory and is considered to be extremely scholarly. He is working, it is said, with the devotion of an archaeologist who has just discovered an ancient tomb. In this case, the cache consists of every old Soviet intelligence file in U.S. possession, some dating back to the Cheka, the original Bolshevik secret police. Months on end are spent reviewing each case. As a result, there is a definite dichotomy in play. Whereas the prevailing spirit in our department is one of pessimism — each day's work threatens to reveal yet another disaster — the exact opposite is true of the Soviet division, where optimism is the order of the day, and each new defector will provide insight into the operations of our enemy. That is why they believe Goltisyn should be their property and, precisely the reason that JJ vows never to relinquish him.

After all, Golitsyn is a real breakthrough for JJ, and the intel — if it is to be believed — making its way down the line becomes more astonishing by the day. There is talk of revelations about the most senior leaders in other governments, including some of our oldest and most trusted partners in the Cold War: Great Britain and Canada.

But maybe the most interesting information to emerge is the details of Golitsyn's defection as relayed by Frank Friberg, our Finland chief. Apparently, Anatoliy showed up on Friberg's doorstep at 6 p.m. on a Friday afternoon. Frank was shaving upstairs at the time when the doorbell rang and had to rush downstairs, half-dressed, to answer the door. Why no one else was available to get the door is not known. Regardless, Frank is confronted by a stocky little Ukranian perched on his doorstep along with his wife and daughter demanding "aswl."

Aswl? I ask with a frown. What's that?

Swedish for asylum, I'm told. According to reports, he resembles more of a Ukrainian peasant, not unlike Khrushchev, round-faced, with close-cropped black hair. It is said that his 15-year career to that point is little more than a number of dreary postings but JJ will hear nothing of it. Golitsyn claims that he was disillusioned with communism, but it is now common currency that he had mistakenly taken the wrong side in a dispute between the ambassador and the resident KGB agent, having backed the ambassador. Nonetheless, it has broken a multi-year drought of defectors for our side and JJ has latched on to him with a tenacity heretofore not witnessed. Some people have likened his determination to hold onto this prize as something akin to the

Battle of Stalingrad — indeed an ironic reference — in regard to JJ's stubbornness and tenacity on the matter.

I am part of the Secret Investigation Group, SIG, a small elite unit of eight set up to unearth evidence of moles in the Company, except since Kennedy's inauguration, my sole job has been investigating the president's activities. In effect, I have become one of JJ's trademark secret units within a secret unit. Even Scotty Miler, the defacto deputy chief, doesn't know what my task is, although he is constantly trying to find out.

When I question JJ as to why he had chosen me for this task his answer is not reassuring.

You believe in Kennedy, so I know you will do everything you can to protect him.

I begin to stutter objections to this generalization but am cut short.

It will give any evidence you unearth greater credibility, JJ responds, waving off my protest.

Greater credibility with whom? I wonder.

A tiny smile forms at the corners of JJ's large, expansive mouth, and his mocha-colored eyes seem to recede even more behind his oversized glasses, but further assurances, alas, are not forthcoming.

Nonetheless, I have been occupied during this time — thankfully, not spending endless hours tediously studying the Trust and Rote Kapel.

Instead, JJ has sent me back to L.A. to track down more information on Judith Campbell, who, it turns out, is a person of interest to a growing number of people, including the FBI.

JJ's personal contact in the federal bureau, Sam Papich, shares some interesting intel with me.

Apparently, after the FBI got wind of Judith Campbell's relationship with the president — could it be JJ who tipped them off during a recent fishing expedition with Papich? Regardless, they set up a wiretap at her apartment on Fontaine Avenue in West L.A. while also instituting around-the-clock surveillance on it, for what purpose even the agents initially involved weren't entirely sure.

Eventually it pays off when the bureau operatives observe two young men entering her apartment through a sliding glass door, where it is discovered, after the pair have left, that they have set up their own listening devices.

The agents on the scene are stunned by this development and want to report this illegal entry to the Los Angeles Police Department, but when they check with their supervisors, the idea is nixed because it would compromise their own ongoing activities.

Nonetheless, the FBI manages to track down the culprits, who are identified through records of a rented car used by them, which turns out to have been booked by a certain I.B. Hale of Fort Worth, Texas. That info causes a bit of a stir because Hale is a former FBI special agent who is now in charge of security for General Dynamics, a company that became heavily involved in the manufacture of military aircraft, having purchased Canadair, a civil and military manufacturer from the Canadian government some time ago after the war.

However, according to sources, business has not been good of late for General Dynamics which is desperate to land the navy's immensely lucrative TFX contract. The company is said to have lost $600 million in the past two years and will stop at nothing to get the $6.5 billion TFX deal.

It appears that former FBI agent Hale had instructed his twin, twenty-one-year-old sons, Bobby and Billy, to plant listening devices in Campbell's apartment and that their efforts have borne fruit as General Dynamics subsequently lands the much-sought-after contract despite major opposition from the navy and overt opposition from our secretary of defense, Robert Strange McNamara.

Not surprisingly, JJ wants all the details, including a briefing on what the FBI had been hearing through its wiretaps when the president calls Campbell.

Mostly small talk about various people, I tell him.

Like whom? he persists.

Frank Sinatra, among others.

Oh, Sinatra. How did those conversations go?

Well, you know he introduced Judith to JFK.

Yea, probably at the direction of the Mob…Giancana.

Don't know about that, I respond.

JJ draws heavily on his cigarette and exhales, all the while deep in thought, before nodding to me to continue.

I don't know what else to tell you, I confess. He just wanted to know all the dirt on Frank, who she's seeing, stuff like that.

Really…how does she respond?

Well, she tells him she's not really in Frank's loop anymore and…

I let the thought drift off into thin air.

C'mon? JJ demands, sensing some reticence on my part to continue.

Well, I hesitate, searching for the right words for an explanation. It appears that she told the president that Frank had once brought another woman into bed with her and had wanted her and the other lady to get it on.

Oh. I suppose that squelched any ideas that the president might have had along those lines.

Ah, I suppose so…certainly, our FBI source was pretty disgusted with all of that, particularly that the president would be so interested in such crap, but the agent was told in no uncertain terms that Hoover wanted every bit of it.

Oh, you can be sure of that, JJ acknowledges.

I'm just about to leave when it occurs to me that I had forgotten some more important and equally compromising information gleaned through the FBI wiretaps.

It appears, I tell JJ, that General Dynamics is not the only company with a financial interest in the president.

Really, he responds with a quizzical grin.

Apparently, Campbell is back to handling money on the president's behest only he's now on the receiving end.

What! JJ exclaims.

I'm sorry. I guess it slipped my mind because of all of this Sinatra stuff.

Well, c'mon, give me the goods, he demands.

It seems that Campbell meets with this guy, a Richard Ellwood, on a regular basis. He's a vice president of some small electronics company in Culver City.

And?

He is giving her money, which she delivers to the president whenever she meets with him.

So, what's the money for? JJ asks.

Not sure what exactly the deal is, other than what the FBI overheard the president advising Campbell that it wouldn't be a bad idea for her to invest some money in this electronics company because there are some good times ahead for it. And…

There's more? JJ exclaims with some agitation.

Ah, the FBI hasn't got it all nailed down yet but yes, some other money is being passed through Campbell to the president from a company that was successful in landing a couple of projects.

Like what?

One was for an unmanned vehicle on land, another had something to do with a water desalinization project, and the third was, um…for avionics for a fighter plane.

What the hell, JJ explodes.

I am shaken by his outburst in part because I can't believe I have allowed myself to become so distracted by the seamier, sexual escapades of the president as to have almost overlooked this more critical information.

There's more than just money changing hands, I confess.

Good God, he exclaims.

Some kinda documents, technical data.

JJ is stunned.

What else are you holding back, he accuses.

Nothing, I stutter, I don't know how I ah….

He waves me out of the office dismissively.

Some time passes before I hook up with JJ again. During that interval, I worry excessively about whether he has lost confidence in me or if it has more to do with the obvious decline in his appearance and behavior.

There are increasing whispers about it in the halls, and I don't know whether it is just my imagination, but people seem to stop talking when I appear on the scene. It is very unnerving, particularly since JJ is not known for being away from the office for extended periods of time.

Suddenly, he is back. I arrive one frosty February mid-morning to find him delving through more files. He barely looks up when I enter and then only to utter one word: Golitsyn.

I sit and watch him for what seems like the longest time, although it may only be about 10 minutes. Finally, he closes the remaining files, re-sorts the ever-present index cards, and shuffles them into a neat pile.

He lights a cigarette and puffs away on it in a perfunctory manner, indicative of one of his increasingly distracted states of late.

Anatoliy Klimov.

I shrug at the mention of the name, indicating my lack of familiarity with it.

JJ is oblivious to my response.

He picks up a file and starts to peruse some of the cards in it.

Anatoliy Klimov is the cover name used by Anatoliy Mikhalovich Golitsyn while stationed in Helsinki, Finland. Late last year, he defected with his wife and daughter and has been here in the U.S., as you know, at an undisclosed location just outside of the Washington area ever since, except for a brief trip to England.

I nod, more as a formality than anything else.

JJ continues. In the past few days, the KGB sent instructions to fifty-four senior agents throughout the world in an attempt to minimize the damage resulting from Golitsyn's defection.

How do we know that? I ask.

It's not important, JJ responds with a scowl.

But you should know this — in the wake of this defection, Vladimire Semichastny…

The KGB chief, I ask?

Right, he has approved a plan for the assassination of Golitsyn and other Soviet traitors, including Igor Gouzenko, Nikolai Khokhlov, and Bohdan Stashnysky. They have also made significant efforts to discredit Golitsyn by promoting disinformation that he was involved in illegal smuggling operations.

Wasn't Khokhlov the fellow who refused to wack some guy who headed up a Russian splinter group in Germany in the fifties?

Mmmm, JJ murmurs, then proceeds to read from a card.

Nikolai Evgenievich Khoklov was a war hero who served behind enemy lines impersonating a Nazi officer. He was responsible, in part, for the assassination of Wilhelm Kube, the Nazi Gauleiter of Belarus.

I nod in agreement, and JJ continues.

However, when Moscow sent him to Germany to co-ordinate the murder of George Okolovich, chairman of the National Alliance of Soviet Solidarists, he….

Didn't his wife talk him out of it? I interject.

Yes, yes, JJ nods in agreement, all the while exhibiting some degree of displeasure at my constant interruptions. Apparently, she told him she didn't want to be married to a murderer.

But he'd already killed people.

That was during the war, this was different.

Where is he now? I ask.

That's not important, JJ responds.

But his wife is said to be in prison in Russia, I add.

JJ nods.

I don't know Stashnysky or Gouzenko, I admit.

Bohdan Stashynsky is also a minor player in terms of strategic value. He was a hitman and, like Khoklov, defected when his wife found out what he was up to and gave him an ultimatum.

Where would we be without Russian wives? I banter.

JJ nods his head in resignation.

So why are those two being lumped in with Golitsyn, who not everyone believes is a significant acquisition?

That seems to stump JJ momentarily.

Finally, after some consideration, he continues.

I think it's more about sending a message to their own people, that regardless of how trivial one might be — and I am not accepting the idea that Golitsyn is anything less than what I think he is — if you cross over, you do so at your peril.

I would think any Soviet with the least bit of common sense would understand that, I venture. It doesn't seem to matter whether you're loyal or not; the slightest pretext can result in you disappearing for years, if not forever.

Clearly, JJ is not amused.

Well, he continues, trying to re-establish his earlier thread. The same can't be said for Gouzenko.

Why is that? I've never heard of him.

JJ grimaces at my apparent ignorance. Igor Gouzenko is the first defector to give us the heads up that the Soviets had planted sleeper agents in our midst.

You mean moles.

Precisely. When he defected in Canada in 1945, he brought numerous files with him exposing Russian espionage activities in the West. You could say his defection signaled the start of what we now call the Cold War.

And he was stationed in Canada?

At the Soviet embassy in Ottawa.

And he was a high-ranking official?

At this point, JJ is becoming exasperated.

No, no, no, he says disgustingly, he was a cipher clerk.

I have some difficulty concealing my astonishment.

A cipher clerk with access to Soviet activities in other countries?

That doesn't strike you as odd?

Not really, JJ responds, but he appears to be on a less-firmer footing than normal. He sorts through some cards to re-establish his line of thought.

Canada was a minor player in terms of espionage in those days — still is in that respect — and I suspect the Russians thought they could store valuable information there without cause for concern. Besides, they almost caught him before the Canadians could effectively provide asylum.

Oh?

Apparently, when he presented himself to the Canadian authorities, the, ahh…the Mounties didn't believe him.

I guess not, I interject, he was only a cipher clerk.

You're trying me, JJ warns.

Okay, I respond. So, what happened?

After some contemplation and a few puffs on his ever-present cigarette, JJ resumes his narrative.

Gouzenko decided to defect because he learned he was being shipped back to Russia and that was the last place, I can assure you, that he wanted to be at that point in time. If you think all the stories we hear now of repression and shortages are bad, imagine what it was like just after the war in a country that already was on the brink of collapse before the Nazis began burning and pillaging the countryside during the invasion and again while in retreat.

I suppose, I concur weakly.

So, JJ continues, he gathers all these files, gets his family together, and heads off to see the, ahh, the Canadian police, the Mounties…

The Royal Canadian Mounted Police, I interrupt yet again. I believe their motto is: We always get our man.

Oh, so we're a comedian today, JJ says with disgust.

I merely shrug my shoulders.

JJ glares at me but continues.

So, he's more or less turned aside by the Canadians …

Then what?

Well, Gouzenko goes back to a neighbor's home where he has stashed his family, and while he's there, he watches a Soviet security team break into his residence.

Oh, I respond with new interest.

Uhuh, JJ nods. Apparently, they turned it over thoroughly looking for the documents.

Do we have independent verification of this?

I don't know, I suppose so, he says resignedly.

So, all's well, that end's well?

Gouzenko's still alive, somewhere in Canada, JJ says, and the Russians would like to get their hands on him, even though this all happened about seventeen years ago.

If we're to believe what we're hearing from Golitsyn, I add, this Gouzenko guy sounds somewhat questionable.

The truth is always complicated when it comes to defectors, JJ responds with a sense of what seems like resignation.

Later at night, I get a call from JJ. I wonder if he's been drinking harder than usual again, as that's typically the case when he has called me previously at this hour. I think Cicely is away yet again on one of her extended absences, although it's increasingly difficult to know as I hear less and less from JJ about his personal life.

After some incidental small talk, he gets right to the point.

You seemed to be harboring some reservations about Golitsyn when we talked today.

That catches me off guard, and I stumble for words for a few moments.

JJ begins breathing harder into the phone, waiting for me to gather my thoughts together.

Finally, I just blurt out what's been on my mind since the news of the defection.

You don't think it's possible that Golitsyn is a plant?

After a long pause, punctuated by even heavier breathing, JJ wearily allows that anything is possible. You have to remember, he reminds me, that even if Golitsyn is a plant, there is useful information to be gleaned from him, intel that would make us want to believe the whole story. And, even if we suspect otherwise, we have to go through the process of making the Soviets believe that we have swallowed the hook.

There's a long silence at the other end which leads me to believe that JJ is either replenishing his beverage or devouring the remainder of it.

Are the Russians really as devious as we've allowed ourselves to believe them to be? I finally venture.

What do you mean? A suddenly alert JJ counters.

I start stammering again, wishing I had a better command of my concerns from a factual basis rather than just increasingly nagging doubts.

Ah, I, ah, just, just can't help thinking that it's all so convenient that Golitsyn has landed in our lap at this juncture.

Convenient? He thunders.

Maybe that's the wrong choice of words, I quickly backtrack.

We can't afford to be wrong, he exclaims, whether it's your poor choice of words or how we handle the information we receive.

The distinctive click at the other end tells me JJ has hung up.

JJ has returned from yet another session with Golitsyn, and his mood is darker with revelations about foreign politicians such as British Prime Minister Harold Wilson and his Canadian counterpart, Lester Bowles Pearson.

Isn't Pearson the guy who won the Nobel Peace Prize for brokering peace over the Suez Canal? I ask.

That's right.

And you believe Golitsyn? Find his accusations credible?

As I've told you before, it's not just a question of whether I believe him or not. It's not as simple as that, he adds, pausing to draw deeply on yet another Virginia Slim. By the time he continues, he is almost enveloped in smoke.

It's incumbent upon me, upon us all, to investigate each and every one of these matters. It's not like everyday life, where we can sweep inconvenient truths or concerns under the rug and pretend they don't exist. We have to examine each minute detail closely, with microscopic precision, if you will, to make sure that we are not overlooking anything that might adversely impact the security of our country, much less the western way of life.

Besides, he pauses, and a strange, painful look momentarily crosses his face.

I…he pauses again…I am in the process of investing in Golitsyn a great deal of the hard-won capital that I have amassed over the years. Hopefully, it will pay off. Otherwise, he pauses to clean his glasses, I may be bankrupt, a spent force.

Both of us sit there quietly for the longest time, mulling over the ramifications. Eventually, I just slip out of the room without a word, leaving JJ in what almost appears to be a catatonic trance.

Nonetheless, JJ's attachment to an individual, who many in our service are now actively referring to as a minor and otherwise undistinguished KGB officer, is worrisome. I subsequently learned that many of his most outrageous claims have never been proven and, in particular, his claims about moles in our ranks may have come out after JJ gave him unprecedented access to British and U.S. files, a course of action he has denied to many others in the past, including Dulles.

Clearly, JJ believes him to be a brilliant scholar with an unusual gift for the analytical. "His mind, without question, is one of the finest of an analytical bent." JJ has been heard to observe. "He is very precise in terms of what he states to be fact, and he separates the fact from speculation."

I could only wish to be that certain.

I am back on the trail of the president and his many women, principally Marilyn Monroe but increasingly Mary Meyer. Monroe had faded somewhat into the background until her emergence at the president's birthday party in late May at Madison Square Gardens provoked yet more countless rounds of speculation.

Her breathless rendition of 'Happy Birthday, Mr. President,' has many shaking their heads, particularly after Kennedy refers to it in public as "sweet" and "wholesome."

There is increased concern when it is learned that her appearance at the party was anything but coincidental and that Bobby had played hardball with Hollywood studio heads who didn't want Marilyn to leave the set on the West Coast of her latest film just to appear at the president's party.

The movie *Something's Got to Give* — an appropriate title, as later events confirm — is a troubled production in no small part because of Monroe. Although cast in the lead role, she has been absent, reportedly, from the set for twenty-two of the thirty-five days it has been in production.

Shortly after her return from New York, 20th Century Fox dismisses her and launches a half-million-dollar lawsuit against her. As a result, Monroe's behavior becomes increasingly erratic. Messages are flying back and forth across the country between the president's brother-in-law, Peter Lawford, and the White House.

There is some thought that Monroe may go public about her relations with the two Kennedys, but that is all put to rest with her sudden death on August 5.

Is it true, JJ asks me, that Lawford was actually talking to her on the phone when she died and that her last words were: "Say goodbye to the president."

I shake my head nervously. Nobody has anything hard and fast on that, to the best of my knowledge, I tell him.

He seems disappointed.

Mary Meyer is an altogether different matter. Since the summer, she has been constantly in the president's company, even at the White House. Dave Powers, the president's designated pimp, has taken the lead role in signing her in on countless occasions, using the notation on the logs: "Powers plus one."

But the most comprehensive information comes from JJ himself, who not only knows Mary well — in addition to being Cord's ex-wife, she is a friend of JJ's wife, Cicely — but he also has instructed subordinates to install bugs in her new home.

My job is to transcribe the tapes, a laborious task made even more difficult by the many notables in her life as well as her ongoing relationship with the abstract-minimalist painter Kenneth Noland. Among the celebrity cast that JJ also wants detailed notes on are *Washington Post* owner Kathryn Graham and journalist Ben Bradlee, who is married to Mary's sister, Tony, both of whom are also acquaintances of JJ.

There are times when I wonder whether any of this info will serve any useful purpose other than titillating JJ and those individuals he keeps on his routing list.

What do I need to know about her? I ask JJ when he puts me on the job.

Where do you want me to start? JJ responds.

I can only smile.

Okay, he says with a sigh. Let's take it from the top.

For starters, she knew the president when she was in college. Met him at a dance and may have been introduced by one of his sisters. The exact details escape me now. By the way, Mary knew my Cicely at Vassar. They were classmates.

She married Cord after the war. By all accounts, it was a relatively happy marriage until the early fifties....

Happy with Cord? I ask somewhat incredulously.

As happy as can be, JJ responds although, I suppose there were signs of, ah, trouble.

Oh?

Well, Mary and Cord hooked up before Cord was injured in the war.

So, what about his lost eye?

His left eye. Shrapnel. JJ grimaces.

They both had pacifist views when they married in '45. At least, that's what Cord led Mary to believe. Both attended the UN Conference...the one in San Fran that led to the founding of the United Nations.

Oh?

Cord was an aide of Harold Stassen, and Mary was supposedly covering the conference as a reporter for a newspaper syndication service. I can't remember or don't know which one. It doesn't matter.

I lean forward to signal my interest in hearing more.

Well, JJ pauses to take a swig from the coffee mug, which increasingly, I suspect, has little familiarity with its namesake beverage. Cord became president of the United World Federalists in 1947. By the way, Albert Einstein was an enthusiastic supporter and even helped raise funds for the organization. In that role, Cord regularly visited colleges and universities, encouraging support ...

JJ catches himself with a smile.

And, enjoying, I am given to understand, the benefits, if you can call it that, of being a disfigured war hero.

The benefits?

Well, apparently many a young, sweet thing took pity on this war hero who now saw the error of his ways.

Took pity?

C'mon. You know what I mean. There were many willing to assuage his pain, ah, physically.

Oh?

Yea, interestingly, I suppose this kind of success led to expectations on Cord's part.

Success?

Well, apparently, even if Mary was with him, he would contact some of the favorable young ladies later to arrange a meeting or two.

Not unlike our president.

Well, not quite like him, c'mon now.

JJ pauses again, to ease his parched throat as well as light yet another cigarette.

At some point, JJ continues, he came to our attention.

Allen claims it wasn't until '51, but it wouldn't surprise me if it was much earlier.

Why?

The narrative was that Cord had seen the error of his ways.

Oh, so it wouldn't look as good if he had always been an anti-Peacenik.

Well, JJ allows, it would have certainly helped him when he came into the cross-hairs of McCarthy.

Oh, right. Allen and Helms had to vouch for him at some point.

That's right! Anyways, he became the principal operative of Operation Mockingbird.

Mockingbird?

Yes, it was a covert operation intended to sway some of the print and broadcast people.

You know, Mary might have been helping him at the time, although her tendency to spur-of-the-moment affairs surely would have made Allen wary of her.

Oh, but Cord's similar proclivities didn't concern Allen?

Well, Cord was a man and Allen certainly wasn't monogamous...not always.

And you? I find myself blurting out.

JJ draws up in offense.

I may not have given my Cecily as much as she deserves. But my indiscretions, if you must, were not those of lust or even amore...they were more failures of attention. You know, the job, it requires so much of my energy, my attention that often little is left for those who truly deserve it...wife, family, and such.

Then...he pauses, adjusting his glasses while contemplating where his narrative will lead us...something happened, and both she and Tony ended up in Europe.

This was before Tony had met Ben Bradlee. In fact, I think she met him in Europe.

JJ pauses again.

Anyway, they both left their husbands and families...I think their mother gave them money for the trip as well as their return fare...which allowed them to spend the entire summer in Europe.

Oh, thank you, Mommy, I interject.

JJ scowls but continues.

Apparently, Mary met some Italian guy, and from that point onward, she really didn't want to have anything more to do with Cord.

But they stayed together...?

If I recall properly, she told him on her birthday about her Italian lover.

A present to herself? I venture.

I know you don't like Cord, JJ responds defensively.

But you do, I declare.

I try not to judge people entirely by whether I like them or not, JJ answers brusquely.

I liked Philby a lot. I hate to think what it has cost our country, much less myself.

I am silent momentarily as I digest this rare instance of introspection from JJ.

But you do like Mary?

JJ lights yet another cigarette and looks away as he blows smoke.

My thoughts or feelings regarding her are of no concern in the matter, he allows. What is important is what's happening with the president.

If my past knowledge of Mary is any guide, she will try and influence him. In what manner, however, we don't know…

I must have a goofy expression on my face because JJ responds with the obvious:

That's your job, to see what you can find out.

So, you're not just interested in the fact that the president is screwing her.

JJ is furious.

I could care less who he screws. Judith Campbell, Marilyn Monroe, Angie Dickenson, Fiddle and Faddle — by the way, Cord is screwing one of them…

Fiddle or Faddle, I ask?

One of them, but I can't remember which one.

I laugh nervously at the irony of Cord Meyer screwing the same woman as the president, who is also screwing Cord's ex-wife; fortunately, it seems to break the tension that had been mounting.

JJ continues.

Mary is also friendly with Jackie, or at least was back in the fifties when the Kennedys lived next door to the Meyers.

Right before Bobby moved there.

JJ ignores that comment.

She also has diaries.

Diaries?

JJ nods.

She's shown them to you?

Of course not, but she's told others about them and…

You've read them? I ask incredulously.

That's not important right now, JJ responds, somewhat defensively.

Besides, with Golitsyn and other stuff on my plate, I don't have time to keep up with Mary and her amorous adventures. That's what you're here for…

Apparently, I'm not the only one working on the Mary Meyer file.

About two weeks later, JJ calls me to join a meeting in progress. I arrive to find him deeply engaged in a discussion with someone with whom I am not familiar. No introductions are extended, but it is clear that this third party has some fairly extensive knowledge about a Company project, which he refers to as MK-Ultra and which involves thousands of experiments with various drugs. The designation, in itself, is interesting as the MK part refers to our Technical Services Division, which leads me to believe he is in that department, while the Ultra has traditionally been used to designate projects of the utmost secrecy.

A little sleuthing around on my part later turns up the information that MK-Ultra was started at the behest of Allen Dulles, hence JJ's connection.

JJ indicates that his visitor should bring me up to speed as to how it relates to what I have been working on.

I suppose, he says somewhat reluctantly, looking at me.

I've been updating Mr. Angleton about our connection with Sandoz.

The Swiss pharmaceutical firm?

Yea, that's right, he responds hesitantly.

Understandably, I am confused as to its connection to Mary Meyer, but he continues.

As you probably know, among other things, they make a special substance.

Substance?

Ahhh, drug, he stumbles.

I shrug my shoulders and look at JJ for guidance.

We're their biggest customer…. He interjects.

Probably their only legal customer, the mystery man says with a laugh.

It's…what did you call it? JJ tries to continue.

Lysergic acid diethylamide, the mystery guest answers.

I look blankly at both of them.

LSD, JJ interjects.

You mean the stuff that guy Timothy Leary has been blathering about? I ask.

More than just talking about it, the mystery visitor notes.

Whaddaya mean? I stammer.

JJ jumps in.

Mary knows Leary. She's used it with him, and we have reason to believe that she has used it with the president, as well.

You mean we've been supplying the president with mind-altering drugs?

No, ah, I wouldn't want to characterize it quite that way, JJ responds hesitantly.

We set up Leary to do this experiment a while back. At the time, Leary was not involved with Mary, nor was he supplying her with the stuff.

But now you think that the president's using it?

Not just him, the mystery man jumps back in.

It's quite possible that other members of the family, Ethel Kennedy for one, may be using it as well.

And Bobby?

Don't know.

He pauses, then shifts gears.

Also, Henry and Clair Booth Luce...

The Time-Life people?

At this point, JJ picks up the narrative.

We've been using Luce and his correspondents to gather some low-grade intel for us for some time now.

Using LSD?

That's more recent, JJ explains. Apparently, it can be quite useful at parties and such.

And Mary has access to it? I inquire

That's right, the mystery man concurs. Leary's been making it available for her personal use.

So, JJ jumps in, I wanted you to know about this so that if you hear or see anything of interest, you'll be able to make a connection.

I nod my head somewhat unconvincingly.

With that, JJ signals an end to my participation in the meeting.

As I start to leave, he looks at me with a smirk.

There was a time when Clair Booth Luce and the president knew each other very, very well.

You mean recently? I ask.

Oh, no…many years ago, in London, I believe, during the time his father was the ambassador, JJ responds.

Maybe I am getting worn down by the day-to-day grind of listening to tapes of private lives, but there are times when I start fantasizing about things that I am not really privy to, such as Mary and the president together: Making love, smoking dope, or dropping LSD.

Am I hallucinating?

Her voice is soft and seductive: Mr. President, would you like to experience how it feels to be outside of yourself, away from the pain you experience, the pressure that grinds you down, the knowledge that haunts you?

He doesn't respond but holds out his hand, and she passes him several tabs.

Each one will take about a half-hour to hit, she tells him, and it will come suddenly and irresistibly.

You've used this stuff? He asks.

Yes, she reassures him. There will be soft, fibrous avenues of light emitting from a central point. We will see the past and the future…

The telephone rings, snapping me back into the present, and after fielding the call, I return to listening to tapes.

Many of the conversations involve the artist Ken Noland, who is enthused about his particular method of choice for escaping the harsh realities of life.

Noland, I have learned, is a disciple of William Reich, a Marxist psychoanalyst from Germany who died in prison here in America in the fifties.

Not surprisingly, JJ is intrigued when I mention Reich to him.

I never cease to be amazed by the breadth of JJ's interests and knowledge.

Reich was in some sort of dispute with the FDA, he tells me.

At first, I think he means FBI but it quickly becomes apparent that JJ's referring to the Food and Drug Administration.

Reich constructed these, ah, I believe they are called orgone boxes…

Orgone?

JJ closes his eyes as if visualizing the boxes.

They were metal-lined, closet-like, he tells me. Patients would sit in them and spend time supposedly absorbing energy. That's how he came into conflict with the FDA. The therapy relied on a series of sessions aimed at removing people's emotional blocks with physical as well as intellectual stimuli.

I look mystified, but JJ continues.

It's a therapy that had a great deal of appeal for women whose husbands had been in the war.

Like Mary, I interject.

Precisely, JJ continues.

The whole idea is to make people less inhibited.

In terms of sex?

Well, of course, JJ continues. According to Reich, the first cause of neurosis is moral inhibition and its driving force — unsatisfied sexual energy.

Is the president a disciple of Reich's? I laughingly query.

If he was, JJ responds, half-seriously, it was well before the Fifties.

Then he smiles.

I think the president is a disciple of his father. You know the stories about old Joe and his affairs with various women, including the actress Gloria Swanson.

JJ stops and laughs out loud.

I look at him quizzically.

I'm just remembering a story that Lyndon told me…

LBJ?

Right. He and Lady Bird were in Palm Beach, after his heart attack, a few years back. Anyways, he was giving a speech about some cause close to Rose Kennedy's heart, and she invited them back for lunch along with Florida Senator George Smathers, a family friend, and an LBJ colleague.

So, they're sitting there eating and who walks in but the old man himself with some seventeen or eighteen-year-old, if that, on his arm. Walks right in, past everyone without a 'Hi,' or 'How are yah?' and heads upstairs, where quickly it becomes evident that he and the young lady are engaging in some very physical interaction, with no concern as to who hears it.

We both sit there, momentarily distracted by the story.

Back to Reich, I prod JJ.

There's not much else to tell, he says.

Reich's dead, but apparently, his advocates live on.

Among Mary Meyer's friends are the Truits, James, and Anne. Like Ben Bradlee, Mary's brother-in-law, James is a journalist who has moved into senior management with the *Washington Post*. Anne is an artist. To further complicate matters, the Truits are also friends of the Angletons: Cecily, more than JJ.

Anne, Mary, and Cecily all dabble in art, with Anne the more accomplished of the threesome. Still, Mary is actively pursuing this field when she is not involved with the president.

It is common knowledge, JJ tells me, that James Truit is infatuated with Mary.

I have to smile at that reference because, increasingly, I've heard similar stories about JJ, although I find it hard to think of JJ in intimate terms with any woman, including his wife, much less a beautiful young thing like Mary.

It's an unusual friendship, JJ continues, in that it is not uncommon for Mary to meet with James without Anne being present.

It's also apparent that Mary has confided in James about her relationship with the president, and on one occasion, I listen as she talks about having shared marijuana with JFK. When I inform JJ about it, he becomes unusually agitated.

LSD and pot, he declares, taking off his glasses and vigorously cleaning them, a typical sign of dissatisfaction or, on occasion, confusion about an issue.

I suppose it's no worse than drinking to excess, I observe.

JJ's withering glance confirms that I have stepped over the line.

Drink can be controlled, he reminds me. Who knows where these illegal substances will lead you?

I decide it is better to appear to feign agreement rather than risk a further confrontation.

Increasingly, I find myself questioning what I should believe. There is no question that what I have learned about the behavior of the president is disturbing. I don't think that I have turned a blind eye over the years regarding the immorality of some of our senior male officials, but this, this is different. It's more than just amoral. It's a blatant disregard for the sanctity of the position he holds.

Fortunately — I suppose that is a poor choice of words — there are greater concerns on the horizon as it has become known that the president and his brother, the attorney general, are engaging in back-channel diplomacy with Georgi Bolshakov, a Russian journalist, who in reality is a senior member of the GRU, the Soviet Army's Main Intelligence Directorate.

According to files being shared by the FBI, Robert Kennedy has met with Bolshakov on six separate occasions in July alone. The word coming from various sources is that the state of affairs in Cuba is the principal topic, but JJ has other suspicions. For one thing, Bolshakov is apparently telling the Kennedys that there is no plan to increase the buildup of Soviet weaponry in Cuba, even though our surveillance is showing otherwise.

Now, people are asking, how would a Soviet journalist — an oxymoron if one ever existed — have knowledge of, much less the capability of conveying such intel?

Nonetheless, the White House has been exerting considerable pressure on us to curtail aerial inspection of Soviet ships in open waters, but fortunately the White House's attempt to influence this activity stops short of actual orders to that effect. By late August, reports are circulating that upwards of fifty-five Soviet ships have docked in Cuba during the past thirty days, four times more than the total that had been recorded for the corresponding period of time in 1961.

Meanwhile, stories surface of Bolshakov being able to walk right into Bobby Kennedy's inner office despite the protestations of Kennedy's secretary, Angie Novello. He is also a regular visitor at Hickory Hill, the Civil-War-era mansion in McLean, Virginia, which Bobby took over from his big brother. It's such a concern that at one point, our director John McCone told the AG that he would not attend a function on the presidential yacht, Sequoia, if Bolshakov is invited, which some people feel is the wrong approach, albeit a principled one, when it comes to trying to keep track of what these so-called Russian diplomats are up to.

To make matters worse, it's becoming increasingly evident that senior personnel are being treated with contempt by the Kennedys. One such individual, Foy Kohler, a diplomat and a Russian hardliner in Berlin, was at one point threatened with bodily harm by Bobby if he ever did anything that the younger Kennedy considered as hindering the president's agenda.

Aside from raising additional suspicions, this back-channel diplomacy is deemed by practiced hands in the State Department to be extremely dangerous given the inexperience demonstrated by the president and his brother in dealing with the Soviets, particularly during the Vienna summit.

This unorthodox form of diplomacy also serves to increase speculation both here and at the FBI, where it is said that Hoover and his 'friend' as well as supposed successor, Clyde Tolson, are monitoring each new development closely.

It's well known that Hoover is increasingly obsessed with Robert Kennedy because of the attorney general's aggressive campaign to crack down on organized crime. It is also common currency here that the Mob is blackmailing Hoover because of his known homosexual relationship with Tolson. This supposition is reinforced by the recognition that Hoover has never aggressively pursued Mob activities, which in turn only serves to anger his nominal boss, the AG. Still, Hoover has sufficient files on the attorney general, the president, and the family to keep the Kennedys at bay. It's been a Mexican standoff to date, but at some point, something's got to give.

Although no one will say it, the president may be the most vulnerable of the three, particularly if it looks like he might win a second term. For one thing, it wouldn't take much for Hoover to begin circulating some of his precious files to selected members of the press that he has cultivated over the years. Instead of the free ride he got in the 1960 election, Kennedy would find himself constantly beset at critical stages in the campaign by embarrassing disclosures about his personal liaisons.

Also, there's no question, JJ tells me, that the Mob thinks that the Kennedys have reneged on a promise to tread lightly with them during this administration as a payback for all of the assistance provided in Chicago during the 1960 election.

Nevertheless, there have been more contacts between our personnel and Mob officials, particularly Chicago gangster Johnny Rosselli, who is fronting efforts to have Castro assassinated — at least, that's the cover story making the rounds at Langley. Among those that Rosselli sees regularly are William Harvey and David Morales — the latter heads up paramilitary operations out of our Miami office. It's a testy situation, given the growing antipathy between the White House, our people, and the Mob.

When asked about what is happening with the Mob, JJ disavows any knowledge, although I happened to overhear him talking to some unknown individual about an upcoming trip to Chicago. Later, he shakes his head in bewilderment when I innocently inquire whether I will be accompanying him on the trip.

Trip, what trip? JJ declares, letting loose a string of expletives in the process. Something I had never witnessed before.

The Soviets replaced Georgi Bolshakov with Anatoli Fyodorovich Dobrynin, the new Soviet ambassador, as their principal contact person with the White House. The story being circulated is that the Kennedys are displeased with Bolshakov for misleading them about Russia's intentions in a variety of locales.

Ever suspicious, JJ thinks otherwise. He believes that Bolshakov simply had developed too high a profile in the capital and that Dobrynin was brought in to throw us — him in particular — off the scent.

He sees Philby's hand in this maneuver, and repeated trips to discuss this development with Golitsyn do little to dissuade him otherwise.

As well, JJ has heard that the Kennedys also made earlier promises to Khrushchev, through Bolshakov, that there will be no retaliatory action for the Soviet construction of the Berlin Wall.

Such a stance is viewed with great displeasure and apprehension by many in our service, not to mention the military.

There is a noticeable increase in tension as word begins to filter out about a Soviet buildup of arms in Cuba, despite JJ's initial skepticism regarding John McCone, a degree of begrudged admiration surfaces momentarily in his comments as to how our new director is handling his first crisis.

After several weeks of in-house discussion over the Soviet buildup, McCone attempts to ratchet up the pressure on the president by sending him a series of 'eyes-only' memos outlining developments in Cuba. However, the memos seem to be greeted with more skepticism than acceptance.

For its part, the administration is telling one and all that it has received assurances from Khrushchev, principally, we believe, through their earlier communications with Bolshakov, that no offensive weapons have been installed in Cuba, only defensive armaments.

There are whispers in the corridors that a more public approach is needed, and within days, it manifests itself in the person of Ken Keating, a newly elected Republican junior senator from New York, who seems to be surprisingly well-informed about the matter, to the point of suggesting in public forums that we have a "do-nothing president" when it comes to dealing with Cuba. But the real zinger is Keating's accusation that the president is suppressing intelligence about the extent of a Soviet missile buildup on the island.

Under other circumstances, it might be considered somewhat humorous — a recently elected junior senator having information of such import — if the situation wasn't so grave. Finally, the president is forced to address the issue at a mid-September news conference in which he declares: "This country will do whatever must be done to protect its own security and that of the allies."

But by now, it's too late. McCone tells the president that not only have the Soviets installed surface-to-air missiles but that, in all probability, they are also in the process of adding medium-range ballistic missiles to Castro's growing arsenal.

And yet the president continues to maintain until early October that there is no reason to disbelieve what he and his brother surely have learned through back-channel discussions with Bolshakov and Dobrynin.

JJ is livid as more details emerge of what is transpiring.

It can't just be mendacity, he mutters to no one in particular when the small talk, during one of his few excursions outside of the office, turns to what is happening on the Cuba file.

For most of the first two weeks of October leading up to the president's belated declaration that the United States has just learned of the existence of Russian offensive weapons on Cuban soil, JJ had remained behind closed doors, ostensibly following up on yet the latest round of allegations by Golitsyn.

Clearly, he feels the loss of Dulles at these times as Allen always made sure that JJ was in the loop on key files, if not involved in the critical decisions. Now, he is reduced to sitting on the sidelines like the rest of us, grazing on what few scraps of intel are thrown our way. I don't know whether it is in part due to his earlier disdain for McCone, as evidenced by comments he made to one and all when Dulles' replacement was announced, or whether Helms, who has become de facto director, has succeeded in freezing him out of the picture, but the Cuban Missile Crisis, as it is later labeled, appears to be a turning point for JJ. Despite his seniority and title, he is now, for all intents and purposes, an outlier, left to wander the periphery in pursuit of moles and traitors.

To make matters worse, at a critical juncture, McCone is out of the country in France on his honeymoon, albeit accompanied by a team of cipher experts as part of his entourage. The in-house joke is that he is better informed on his honeymoon, thanks to the cipher team, than when he is here at Langley.

The country, dare I say the whole world, has been on tenterhooks for days now as revelations emerge about Russian missiles in Cuba and a looming potential nuclear confrontation.

Like most of our fellow countrymen, JJ and I are forced to follow events on television.

Helms and his associates are holed up in their offices or attending White House meetings. McCone is virtually invisible.

Maybe, JJ allows, in one of his rare light-hearted moods, he is still in honeymoon mode.

The laughter is short-lived.

Watching the president address the nation at the most critical juncture of this crisis, it is hard to envision him as a leader, much less have confidence in his decision-making abilities. Instead, what I see is a man stripped naked, consorting with various and sundry women in lewd and lascivious behavior. It's hard to shake the image that has been created in my mind by successive examinations of his private lifestyle. I suspect I am not alone in that regard.

And what advice is he receiving from his advisors? Are they standing up to challenge his views when necessary, or do they simply remain seated as a White House steward serves yet another bowl of clam chowder to the president and his brother, leaving the rest hungry for respect?

These are difficult images to shake. I think of discussing them with JJ, but I fear he will mock me or, worse still, pretend not to hear my concerns.

He is in a world of his own at this point, increasingly consumed with cigarettes, bourbon, and traitors, real or imagined.

The crisis has passed, or has it?

The word is that the "other guys blinked," but as JJ notes with disdain, only those who truly believe that the world was on the brink of nuclear devastation, or some lesser catastrophe, will be buying that story. I look at him quizzically, but he is clearly too preoccupied to share any confidences.

After the dust clears, JJ sets out to work on what remains of his old contacts to see what he can discover. The most notable source is Dean Gooderham Acheson, who, it turns out, was part of Ex Comm, a strategic advisory executive committee, hence the name, set up by the president during the crisis, ostensibly to provide him with advice. There have been times when JJ had crossed swords with Acheson in the past, particularly early in the Truman administration, when it was thought that Dean might be protecting some communist sympathizers, specifically Alger Hiss, but those days have long passed. Over time, Acheson's and JJ's once divergent views have coalesced. Adding to the intrigue is the knowledge that Acheson's daughter, Mary, is Mrs. William P. Bundy, the wife of a former analyst here at Langley, whose more hawkish brother McGeorge is a key Kennedy advisor. Despite what one might think, given the vast number of individuals working in or for government and the fact that there are elections every second year for Congress, one-third of the Senate, and every fourth year for president, Washington remains a very closed society. Almost in-bred, one might conclude.

Over lunch, Acheson tells us that fellow advisory member Robert A. Lovett, who had succeeded Acheson as undersecretary of state in the late forties and then later served as secretary of defense in the Truman administration, had been treated rather abysmally by the attorney general during the crisis.

At one point, Acheson recalled, Bobby yelled at Lovett, a man who had further distinguished himself in banking and finance after leaving public office.,

It wasn't in anger, Acheson allowed, just simply disrespect.

Yelled at the likes of Robert Lovett, JJ exclaims incredulously.

Acheson nods in acquiescence.

Apparently, Acheson continues with a degree of amazement, the AG didn't know Lovett, so when the president asked Bobby to invite Lovett into the Oval Office, he simply stuck his head out of the door and yelled, "Hey, you!"

When Lovett didn't respond, Bobby yelled a second time.

At that point, somewhat confused, Lovett apparently pointed to himself as if to ask: Me?

Bobby responded with irritation, "Yes, you. Come here."

JJ can't believe it. How did the president respond to this? He asks Acheson.

Acheson shakes his head. He wasn't pleased, but that's not the point.

For JJ, mention of the incident serves to further convince him that the president and his brother are not worthy occupants of such an important public office. It also makes him increasingly wary of the president's motives.

The public consensus, in the wake of the Missile Crisis, is that the president had finally stood up to Khrushchev and the Soviets, but JJ seems skeptical and appears to be pursuing a different scenario. There are more meetings with Golitsyn, more time spent away from Langley and even when he is back, I often see unfamiliar faces entering and leaving his suite.

One thing that is surfacing that disturbs JJ immensely is the apparent disconnect that developed during the crisis regarding outside advisors and the president's key staff.

On the one hand, he tells me, we have McGeorge Bundy explaining why he had delayed advising the president immediately after being given evidence of a Soviet ballistic missile site in Cuba.

Bundy claimed that he thought the president needed a quiet night of sleep and relaxation after an exhausting day on the campaign trail before being presented with information that might require a significant decision. To which JJ snorts: The president probably had a prearranged liaison with Mary or one of his other female companions, and staff were extremely hesitant to disrupt him or his plans, just as had been the case on several other critical occasions.

How's that? I ask.

I have it on good authority, JJ explains, that at the very least, there have been two times when senior military personnel have been dissuaded from presenting critical information to the president because he is otherwise engaged — if you know what I mean. Both instances occurred around the lunch hour and at a time when the first lady was absent from Washington.

And then there's the revelations from Dean Acheson outlining the tenor of discussions of the executive committee of the national security council. Most were pushing for a stronger military response than the blockade, but their efforts were being resisted by the attorney general, who likened such a plan to the attack on Pearl Harbor by the Japanese.

It's almost as if, JJ wonders aloud, that the AG knew that they wouldn't need any stronger action to make the Russians back down.

As expected, there are some scapegoats in the wake of the crisis, and among them is Bill Harvey, who has been replaced by Desmond Fitzgerald. If you believe the White House, the last straw in this tumultuous and difficult relationship between Harvey, the president, and his brother occurred in the lead-up to the crisis when Harvey, as is his wont after a typically large lunch, was caught dozing by the president during a briefing. According to several sources, the president launched a tirade that lasted eight to ten minutes.

Apparently, JJ was talking to General Charles E. Johnson III, the army representative to the group, who described it as the "damnedest" thing he had ever witnessed, adding that Director John McCone was also present and never said a word in Harvey's defense.

However, in checking with Samuel Halpern, who, along with Harvey, acted as our liaison with the White House on Cuba, it turns out that at one point early on during the crisis, Harvey had indelicately pointed a finger directly at the president and his brother and declared: "We wouldn't be in such trouble now if you guys had had some balls in the Bay of Pigs."

Even by Harvey's standards, this was unimaginable. Everyone was stunned, recalls Halpern, who, nonetheless, expressed begrudging admiration: "You don't say that to the president in his own office, but Harvey was the only guy who had the guts to do it."

Word is that McCone, who was again present, wanted to fire Harvey immediately but that Richard Helms convinced him that he should be reassigned, with the rotund agent ending up as chief of station in Rome.

When apprised of the situation, JJ allows that it's further evidence that Helms is now running the show here at Langley.

Halpern, who is with us at the time, nods his head in agreement, although I am not sure whether Sam is part of the increasingly pro-Helms circle and will report this conversation back to Richard.

Nonetheless, when nudged by JJ, he is quite expansive about what is happening on the Cuba file, and in particular Florida where most of the activity has coalesced.

He describes it as a catacomb with layers of Mob and anti-Kennedy connections intertwined with our personnel.

And Richard is the man at the center? JJ posits.

Halpern just smiles at the reference to Helms.

You know Richard better than any of us, he responds. He's as well-informed as anyone can be under the circumstances.

Oh? JJ responds with a raise of an eye.

There are so many layers of intrigue, Halpern continues. There are anti-Castro people plotting with the Mob...

Rosselli? JJ interrupts.

Not just Rosselli, although there's no doubt that he was Bill's man.

JJ merely nods in agreement.

It's an interesting climate down there, he allows.

The other casualty in the post-Cuban Crisis is General Edward Lansdale, previously a favorite of the president due to his exploits in Indo-China. Lansdale had been brought in to give the White House a direct and more secure connection to Operation Mongoose, which from our side had been headed up by Harvey and Halpern but clearly was the pet project of a White House increasingly obsessed with covert action.

In talking to one of Lansdale's underlings, a Daniel Ellsberg, I learned that the White House thought that Lansdale's experience in counterinsurgency during the Huk Rebellion in the Philippines would serve us in good stead in overthrowing Castro.

According to Ellsberg, the operation was being run out of Bobby's office despite the involvement of Harvey and Halpern.

Maybe that explains in part, Harvey and Halpern's deep dislike and distrust for the attorney general, I tell JJ later.

In part, maybe, but not in total, he responds.

Overall, it is estimated that upwards of thirty operations have been planned or considered but none bear fruit.

Either Castro leads a very charmed existence, I begin…

… or we are not as committed to ridding this planet of him as we pretend to be, JJ interjects, finishing the thought.

You mean we, as in here in Langley? I respond in a thunderstruck tone of voice.

Of course not, JJ says dismissively. I meant the 'royal we,' the Kennedys.

Lost in the buildup of tension over Cuba is the crisis brewing at Ole Miss, where a 28-year-old Negro air force veteran, James Meridith, is forcing the segregation issue to the forefront by attempting to enroll at the state university.

Ironically, at a time when the president and the military needed to be working together to defuse the Missile Crisis, the president further exacerbated their relations by calling in the 503rd Military Police Battalion to assist a rag-tag collection of federal officials charged with keeping peace at Ole Miss. The makeup of the group, which included alcohol and tobacco agents, border patrolmen, and hastily deputized prison guards, however, proved to be woefully inadequate for the job at hand, and they found themselves under siege at the university by an estimated force of 2,500 students, Klansmen and, later-confirmed, some off-duty law officers.

The White House was incensed by the lack of speed with which the military police responded to their orders, leaving Meredith and his protectors at risk throughout much of the night.

Army Secretary Cyrus Vance and Major General Creighton Abrams bore the brunt of the president's frustration. It's estimated that the president called at least fifteen times during the night, demanding an explanation as to the lack of progress.

For Abrams, the humiliation is considerable given that he was suffering from a ruptured disc and was forced, literally, to absorb the president's displeasure, laying down on his office floor, all the while being berated over the phone by a president who demanded to know what was taking the army forces so long.

Later, it is learned that members of the 503 were not only inexperienced in dealing with domestic issues but had no idea of how to get to Oxford, Mississippi. At one point, the battalion, in full battle gear, pulled their jeeps into a back-country service station in a desperate attempt to obtain some highway maps. There is even talk that they dragooned a military officer who seemed to have knowledge of the area.

Finally, many hours later, the military police rode to the rescue, but not before the White House had again short-circuited the military line of command, as happened during the Bay of Pigs, by giving direct orders to men in the field.

Some people are suggesting that the plotline in a popular, newly released novel, *Seven Days in May*, in which a faction in the military plots to overthrow the president, may not be so far-fetched given the circumstances and the growing tensions between the top brass and their commander-in-chief.

By December, however, Bobby Kennedy pulled together a private ransom of some $53 million in pharmaceuticals and farm machinery to be paid to the Castro government for the release of Cuban prisoners, but it potentially had an unintended effect. It puts a whole bunch of desperadoes back in the U.S. who believe that the president and his brother abandoned them on the beach at the Bay of Pigs.

JJ seems surprisingly pleased with the development.

The Cubans are schemers, he tells me. And they talk with their hearts rather than their heads, but will they act on their own?

I shake my head to indicate that I don't know.

JJ smiles.

Well, that's one of two possible answers.

Oh, I respond, and the other?

The other is obviously no, JJ states with authority, all the while exhibiting that Cheshire Cat grin of his.

So, I ask him, do you think that all of the anti-president commentary that we have been hearing since the Bay of Pigs is mostly just talk, letting off steam?

Don't misunderstand me, JJ responds. These people are incredibly angry and with good reason, particularly now that the president has promised Khrushchev that we wouldn't attack Cuba, but they need a way to channel their anger into action, and ever since Castro turfed them out of their homeland, the only real action we have seen has been driven by us. On their own, they just sit around and drink and complain, then drink some more.

What about the Mob contacts? I ask. Aren't they capable of spurring action?

No doubt about that, JJ responds after a moment's reflection.

In fact, I think that's the real reason why Harvey had to go but not be fired.

Huh? I respond with a blank look.

JJ takes a swig from a coffee mug that looks to contain something other than coffee or water, then lights another Virginia Slim and inhales deeply.

It's something I've been wondering about, he finally allows.

I wait as, surprisingly, he blows a smoke ring.

Helms had been after Harvey to break off his ongoing contact with Johnny Rosselli, but Harvey, in his own inexplicable way…JJ pauses to smile…simply refused.

Why is that? I ask.

Well, you know Bill, if you say something is black, he thinks it's white.

I laugh. I guess so, I tell him guardedly.

Harvey thinks of Rosselli as a friend or, at worst, an associate.

Oh, really, I respond.

Do you think of your Mob contacts as friends or simply associates?

JJ is clearly disgusted.

He lowers his head, shaking it vigorously.

What do I have to do to dissuade you of these idiotic notions about me and the Mob?

He looks back up and stares intently at me in that way of his that can be very intimidating.

But this time, I am not wavering.

After what seems like an eternity, he lights another cigarette from the one in his ashtray that is only half-finished. He shakes his head yet again, but am I being fanciful in thinking I detect the beginnings of a small smile at the corners of his mouth.

Then, he picks up a file and begins to work his way through it. After a few minutes more of silence, punctuated only by a few grunts of disapproval from JJ as he peruses a file, motionless, his head wreathed in a halo of swirling tobacco smoke, I leave the room.

There are questions being raised about the decision to withdraw 15 Jupiter missiles from Turkey, which was announced by the secretary of defense, Robert McNamara, the day after Khrushchev's supposed capitulation on Soviet missiles in Cuba.

The administration is claiming that there is no linkage between the two, and for the most part, it goes unnoticed both in the press and amongst the public.

However, it's a different matter in the military where already strained relations between the top brass and the president worsened during the Cuban Crisis and the situation in Mississippi.

In all of his public discussions, the president has been very determined to ensure that no one knows that, basically he and his brother acted alone in dealing with the Russians to the point that in an hour-long interview with the three major television networks, the president overtly spreads the falsehood that members of the Ex Comm committee actually helped "hammer out" decisions during the "five or six days" leading up to a resolution of the issue.

JJ becomes increasingly incensed as we watch it on TV.

Outright lies, he mutters while smoking furiously.

He is so absorbed by the fabrications being spread by the president that a drink has been left untouched on the table beside his chair for the better part of the hour.

"After all the alternatives were examined…" the president says near the end, "a general consensus developed…that the course of action that we finally adopted was the right one."

Those final words are uttered just as JJ is lifting the previously neglected drink to his lips. Instead, he slams it down with sufficient force, spilling almost half.

JJ looks at the drink and then at me and shakes his head.

How is he getting away with this?

When I don't respond, he gulps down what is left of the bourbon.

Late in the year, JJ returns from meeting with various members of the Joint Chiefs with the news that apparently, the president's chat with the TV networks, a week before Christmas, has not gone unchallenged.

How's that? I ask.

Ah, well, he begins, they assigned an army lieutenant colonel — he pulls a note from his pocket — Alexander M. Haig Jr., to produce an analytical study of the crisis from a military point of view, including the decision to pull out the Jupiter missiles and the timing of the announcement by McNamara.

And…? I ask.

JJ smiles.

The report states that rather than being coincidental, as the president maintains, it looks more like a "secret arrangement."

And how is that being received?

Well, it depends upon one's perspective, he responds. The Joint Chiefs thought enough of it to send a copy along to Max Taylor, their chairman.

Oh?

I'm told he slammed it down angrily at their next meeting and informed one and all that he would not be transmitting it to the president.

He's not the only one in denial, I add.

That piques JJ's attention.

Apparently, the Secretary of State Dean Rusk met with the Congress the other day and was less than candid in his remarks on the matter.

How's that? JJ wonders.

Well, Senator Hickenlooper of Iowa…

JJ begins to laugh.

Not just any Hickenlooper, he guffaws. That would be Senator Bourke B. Hickenlooper of Iowa, the second-ranking Republican on the Foreign Relations Committee.

That's right, I concur.

Anyway, the senator asks Rusk directly to confirm that the removal of the Jupiters "was in no way, shape or form, directly or indirectly connected" with the Missile Crisis settlement.

And what did Rusk say? As if I can't guess, JJ adds.

Mr. Rusk said: "That is correct, sir."

I thought as much.

I nod my head in agreement.

Sometime later, I tell JJ that McNamara was asked the same question by Senator John C. Stennis, a Mississippi Democrat and chairman of the Senate defense appropriations committee.

And what did he say, JJ inquires, knowing full well the answer.

"Absolutely not," the record states.

In fact, I continue, he told the Senator that when the Soviet government raised the issue, the president absolutely refused to discuss it and that the Russian leader was told in no uncertain terms that members of Ex Comm were contemplating the possibility of launching nuclear weapons.

Well, that's only a half-lie, JJ responds. Ex Comm did raise the issue, but Bobby put an end to it rather quickly, imputing that any such attack would be viewed as not unlike Pearl Harbor.

JJ removes his glasses to clean them.

I don't suppose, he asks, whether anyone on the appropriations committee considered questioning McNamara as to why the announcement was made exactly one day after the crisis ended.

1963

We have to distrust each other.
It is our only defense against betrayal.

It's early in the morning when I encounter JJ in the hallway —
an unusual occurrence in time and place of late. He seems
somewhat agitated and waves to me to come into his outer
office.

You heard about Philby?

I shake my head warily.

He's defected.

When?

Earlier today or late yesterday. I'm not sure which day. You
know, those damnable time-zone differences.

I nod my head in agreement.

So, what happened?

JJ smiles. Clearly, early conversations have been forgotten
or dismissed.

Golitsyn helped us nail him.

If you nailed him, how come he's managed to get away, I
wonder aloud.

That stops JJ momentarily.

Well, you know the Brits, they don't just grab someone, they like to do things...

At this point, he affects an English accent.

...rather proper.

I smile.

They were talking to Philby, he says with some exasperation.

He denied everything, just like in the past. The next thing you know, he's on a Soviet freighter heading to Russia.

A freighter?

Uh huh, the Dolmatova or something like that. It shows up in Beirut, begins to unload its cargo, and then leaves on short notice.

What do you mean? I ask.

Well, according to reports, the crew left cargo scattered on the dock....

You know, it's not like the Russians to waste money or goods.

By the way, I am not the only person who had become overly suspicious of my former good friend.

Oh?

Well, you knew how our James Bond felt.

Our James Bond?

Yea, Harvey.

Oh, Bill. Well, that's no surprise. And is there another person?

Miles Copeland.

Miles? Wasn't he a close friend of Philby's?

Well, we were all fooled to some extent, some more than others.

Yourself?

JJ winces and takes a drag on his Virginia Slim.

Rubbing it in, are we? He finally allows.

I can't suppress the hint of a smile. Fortunately, JJ is too busy stubbing out his smoke to notice.

You know, at one point Miles was forced to fill in an ultra-thorough checklist from a superior, designed to determine if Kim committed any suspicious actions as prescribed by this form.

JJ pauses to gather his recollection.

Initially, he had objected to the idea of spying on Kim because of their friendship but eventually obliged under pressure.

And what were the results?

Again, JJ winces, although there is evidence, ever so briefly, of a small smile.

Well, they were friends....

And?

None of the points in the checklist had been checked.

That mustn't have gone down well.

Now, JJ can't suppress a small chuckle.

Of course not. Miles was admonished by his superior, who said something to the effect that even a normal person would have committed at least one of the suspicious items on the list.

Sensing the need to change the direction of the conversation, I raise the question that I think many are pondering: So, were the Russians tipped off?

I don't know, JJ says with concern. What are you trying to get at?

I can only shrug my shoulders.

You're the expert on this stuff.

Well, he starts to respond with yet another grimace, but nothing follows.

There is an awkward silence, and then he starts shuffling files, which is my signal to leave.

We are at NSA headquarters at Fort Meade, Maryland, a vast glass house surrounded by electric wire fences and topped with the tangled stems of hundreds of aerials and receiver dishes, which link the NSA to its many listening posts around the world.

Along with JJ are Dick Millen and Lish Whitman from the FBI and, back from Italy, Bill Harvey. Harvey had pursued Philby with an implacable vengeance that exhibited a streak of vindictive anti-British sentiment. Included in the British contingent are the Hughs, Alexander and Denham, plus JJ's old friend, Peter Wright.

The Brits are hoping to redeem themselves in our eyes as the taint of the Maclean-Burgess disaster in the fifties takes on new life in the wake of Philby's defection. However, any hope of redemption quickly dissipates in the course of Wright's presentation, which particularly angers Harvey.

It starts with Wright providing a somewhat glib observation. Most espionage is tedious work at best, he allows, involving laborious hours waiting for something to happen.

Wright embellishes his point by noting that, on occasion, they would drink Scotch while on a stakeout.

Silly Brits can't recruit agents directly, Harvey mutters under his breath, noting that Wright had to resign from the navy and then wait six months before being approached by MI5. And, he adds, once they bust a spy, they lose all control of the evidence because it becomes a police matter.

One case, in particular, which rubs everyone the wrong way involves the arrest of a Gordon Arnold Lonsdale, a supposed Canadian, whose cover in Britain was operating a jukebox-leasing business. MI5 searched his flat for nine days and only discovered the location of his transmitter on the last day, hidden in a cavity under the floor along with a camera and other paraphernalia in moisture-resistant sealed packages.

We listened to Lonsdale making love to a woman he had picked up, Wright relates, and then he gets her out in the morning in time for his transmission from Russia.

Lonsdale is assisted by Peter and Helen Kroger, posing as Kiwis, who run a small bookshop specializing in Americana antique books. In reality, they are Morris and Lona Cohen, a pair of Americans wanted by the FBI in connection with the Rosenberg nuclear espionage case.

Wright allows that he is embarrassed because the FBI had asked earlier if they were the Cohens and he had not followed up on it.

Lonsdale also is not as advertised. Turns out he is Konan Trofimovich Molodi, son of a well-known Soviet scientist. He assumed the identify of Lonsdale, a long-deceased Finnish Canadian, in 1955.

In the fall of 1960, British agents follow Lonsdale for short stretches whenever he leaves his office. Each time, they have to pick him up at the spot they left off at — for fear of being spotted — so it takes them two weeks to track him to his home, and they use countless agents and even, on occasion, some wives.

JJ laughs uproariously at the idea that the Brits are so stretched out that they are using wives for surveillance. Later, in a rare social outing with Allen Dulles, JJ relates that particular piece of intel to our former head. Imagine me using my Cecily or your Clover for surveillance, he notes. Allen puts down his corn-cob pipe, stunned at the revelation.

Wright discovered that the Russians knew that the Brits were onto Lonsdale. First, they withdrew him but then sent him back. Why? He asks JJ.

Obviously, JJ concludes, the Soviets wanted to identify one of the moles in their organization so they sacrificed Lonsdale, albeit in vain, in the hopes of getting our agent. But they also had to be concerned about blowing the cover of their mole in MI5, so there was a double purpose to the sacrificing of Lonsdale.

We are all unsettled by what befell Wright when he tried to identify traitors in their midst and reported his concerns up the ladder.

After many months waiting for an official response, Wright explains, I was brought before Deputy Director-General Graham Mitchell and Sir Roger Hollis, director-general of MI5, the Brits equivalent of our FBI.

I, too, have reasons to suspect Hollis, JJ interjects. So, what happened?

Hollis was fingering my report like it was something evil, Wright recalls. He looks at me coldly and announces that

Mitchell, who gives the appearance of being increasingly uncomfortable with the whole mess, will handle the discussion.

Mitchell is sweating slightly and avoids looking me in the eye. At that point, Mitchell allows that it's all rather over his head. In my experience, espionage has always been a simple business, he tells me.

JJ fails valiantly at suppressing a guffaw.

Precisely, Wright says.

You were not pleased, I gather, Peter.

A little steamed, he allows, adding that Mitchell simply dismissed many of the concerns in Wright's report.

And…. JJ responds with one eyebrow raised.

Wright sighs.

Mitchell ignored my arguments. Instead, he stated that the simple fact is that we have arrested and convicted three professional Russian illegals — these are the first Russian nationals to be brought before the courts here for generations. He blathered on about this arrest of two immensely dangerous spies inside the country's most secret underwater research establishment, and that, by any measure, is a success. What on earth, Mitchell observed, is the advantage to the Russians of allowing us to do that?

Oh, my, JJ says softly.

There's silence in the room.

So, you wanted a further investigation?

Yes, I did, Jim. Very much so.

But that was not to be?

Well, no, Mitchell attacked every point I made —

vigorously, I might add.

And you tried to rebut?

Yes, but it was futile. Finally, Hollis jumped back in. He told me that he and the deputy had discussed the whole matter "very carefully," adding he was sure that I was aware of his feelings on that point.

Hmm, JJ responds.

So, I asked, am I to understand that there will be no further investigations?

And who responded at that point? JJ jumps in. Mitchell or Hollis?

Hollis. He told me in no uncertain terms that the matter was to be kept; I think the word he used was "confidential."

And that was that?

Hollis looked at me with a peculiar kind of smile and started sharpening a pencil.

I stood up rather abruptly, I believe, and left the room.

But here in the U.S. we were all very impressed, JJ says, albeit at the same time disappointed.

Naturally, during the meeting with Peter Wright, the conversation turns to Kim Philby, who both knew and, to varying degrees, were fooled by him. It turns out that during Philby's tour of duty in America, JJ had met with him at least 36 times in his office, no less, as the log records Philby visiting there regularly. Then there were the countless lunches, usually once a week at Harvey's. Each time JJ dictated a memorandum to a secretary, Gloria Loomis, recording what was discussed.

But now, there are no records, which is astonishing considering JJ's reluctance to discard any file.

This startles Peter Wright, who queries JJ about the whereabouts of the files, forcing him to admit that they were too embarrassing and are gone.

Gone! Wright confirms incredulously.

Burned! JJ responds. I thought I could drink Kim under the table, but it turned out that all of the under-the-table work was being controlled by Kim.

The sense of betrayal is shattering for me, JJ allows in a rare moment of introspection. It made it impossible to be objective about anybody…and then came Golitsyn.

Oh, yes, Golitsyn, Wright observes. He set you straight, did he?

Well, let's not go overboard, JJ responds. But it turns out that he was correct.

Wright lets that sink in for a moment, then shakes his head wearily.

Nonetheless, for JJ, despite his own suspicious nature and the fact that he considers himself to be a cunning and clever man, the prospect that he was duped and humiliated by Philby is unbearable.

In many respects, Philby was everything that JJ aspired to be, minus the stutter. A product of the privileged old-boy system and being a graduate of Britain's notorious public-school system, which spawned numerous traitors, JJ fell hook, line, and sinker for Philby's upper-class plausibility.

How is it, he had on occasion mused after a few tipples, that Philby could take in such a clever, suspicious person like myself?

Fortunately, no one ever ventured a guess.

Later, we are sitting in La Nicoise in Georgetown, looking to enjoy an after-dinner digestif. As is his wont, JJ reserved table 41, which is situated in front of the rear wall. No one can sit behind him, and it allows him to see everyone in the room.

JJ has already consumed a martini and a kir before dinner, and then copiously partakes of the several bottles of fine claret ordered by Peter to accompany our meal. Now, he has requested a Harper Bourbon with two ice cubes.

The waiter turns to me, and I order a Cutty Sark…also on the rocks.

Ah, just like the Kennedy men, Wright observes.

I nod my head and smile, only to be met by a scowl from Peter.

I wouldn't drink that rotgut if it was the last drop of alcohol on this fair earth, he states with typical British authority.

My jaw drops.

Much less add ice cubes to any self-respecting whiskey, he continues, looking briefly at JJ, who appears to be oblivious to our exchange.

Now, for my money, Wright continues, give me a nice, peaty Laphroaig, he tells the waiter, who immediately sports a frown.

I believe our only single malt is Glenlivet, he responds after some reflection.

Well, better it than Cutty Sark, although it's no great improvement. And, neat, he bellows after the retreating waiter.

After several top-ups and some disjointed conversation that meanders, I bid the pair of them adieu at about 11 p.m., although I am concerned about the prospect of leaving JJ unattended in his current state.

Peter shows up at JJ's outer office later the next morning, looking somewhat the worse for wear and increasingly concerned about JJ.

Jim is drinking far more than is good for him, or me for that matter, and he's begun to look more than merely pallid but genuinely ravaged, he tells me. Also, his mood has changed, has it naught, he asks?

I can only nod my head.

We went for a walk last night, he continues. Good Lord, it must have been after 2 a.m. by then.

My raised eyebrows encourage him to explain.

It was a long, long night, he recalls. I am not sure of how many places we visited and the stories we shared.

Too much to drink, I suppose, he says in his typically understated British manner. Before you know it, we are well past the hour of turning in, and instead, we continue on foot rather than chance driving.

JJ rarely sleeps these days, I remind him.

Yes, he's not alone in that regard.

He seemed increasingly introspective, Wright continues, and that wonderfully dry humor of his has all but disappeared. Is it just me, or does he also seem more aggressive and trusts fewer people?

You're not alone in that interpretation, I tell him.

So, what did you talk about?

The usual. Who's true, who's false. Who really defected, and who was sent. More of the latter in Jim's mind, I daresay.

My silence begs him to continue.

This constant search for traitors is wearing and makes for extended ruminations, but eventually, the alcohol began to wear off, and we headed back to the car by way of the 44th Street Bridge, I believe.

Let me guess, I interject. He parked the car down behind the Okinawa Memorial, near the National Cemetery.

Wright smiles. I must confess to being a touch impressed by the patriotism of you Americans, which manifests itself in so many ways.

Oh?

Take Jim. There is no mistaking his reverence for the flag and symbols of national heritage, such as the Okinawa Memorial. I think we must have stood there for the better part of 15 minutes in silence.

Without a word?

Yes, it seemed endless, but obviously, there was much going through Jim's mind.

What makes you say that?

Peter is quiet for a moment.

I suppose I can tell you, he says after some contemplation.

Yes?

Just before we got int the car, he turned to me and declared, with considerable resignation: It's all Kim's work.

Oh?

That's all, but it's the only time I have ever heard him mention his old, dear friend in that manner.

Well, something along those lines does pop up from time to time, I confess. No question that he is obsessed with what he views to be more than just a betrayal of one's country and friendships.

Yes, yes, Wright says, rather animatedly, a betrayal of ideals and principles. It's so wonderfully old-fashioned, I suppose, and yet....

The thought drifts off into silence as Wright seems lost in some sort of reverie of his own. I nervously shuffle a few papers.

But Peter is not quite finished with recounting the night's escapade.

Continuing, he tells me that they finally ended up at Arlington National Cemetery at daybreak as the early morning commuters began to make their way along the Beltway and into the nation's capital.

I don't know whether it was the amount of drink we had consumed, but it seemed like we sat for the longest time in silence, he says.

Jim seemed transfixed by the endless row of headstones, he continued.

Finally, he started to recite the names of a few of the notables buried there. Presidents Washington and Taft, and some military figure, Pershing.

General Pershing? I ask.

Yes, Peter adds.

Oh, I wonder why?

My sentiments, precisely, Peter responds.

So, you asked him?

I didn't need to. He started rambling on about his father serving under General John J. 'Black Jack' Pershing in some kind of Mexican thing without which he wouldn't have been here.

And you asked him about it?

It took a bit of prying — probably because of the amount of drink we had consumed — but he finally allowed that in the course of his service, Jim's father met his mother in some small town on the Arizona border.

Nogales, I tell him.

I think so, he responds. My abilities were not all that they should be at that point, I suppose.

That would make sense and hence his middle name, Jesus, I note. Did he say anything else?

Hmm, Peter says. Something about wanting to be buried there someday.

Oh? Nogales?

No, Arlington. But then he added he was sure the leadership would never want to reveal all of what he'd done and, of equal importance, what he hadn't been able to do.

My bewildered look encourages Peter to expand, but all I receive in return is silence as Peter stares vacantly into space.

He didn't say anything further?

Peter shakes his head.

No, we sat there for another 15 or 20 minutes — who knows for sure how long — then, Jim abruptly stood up, headed for his car, and likely would have left me stranded if I hadn't gathered my wits together sufficiently and scurried after him.

From there, it was back to my hotel and God knows where he was off to — I don't suppose he has shown up yet.

Not a word, I tell him but that's not entirely abnormal of late. Increasingly, he has not been showing up at the office until sometimes even mid-afternoon.

Oh, really? Peter responds.

Yes, ever since Dulles was forced out and their early morning ritual of fishing tales ended, his routine has become increasingly erratic, to say the least, I tell him.

Peter shakes his head several times.,

I suppose I should be off, he says finally with a quick glance at his watch. Bags to pack, a plane to catch.

Then he is gone.

I arrive at the office around noon to find JJ pouring over newspaper reports in both the *New York Times* and the *Washington Post* about a speech given by the president at American University here in Washington.

Not content with just the stories that had appeared in the papers, he has already asked for and received a copy of the speech, and there is said to be equal interest in the president's remarks at both the Pentagon and the FBI.

What sets this speech apart is the president's attitude about communism.

Don't you find it odd, JJ says, given all of what transpired last fall — the world being on the brink of a nuclear catastrophe — that the president is now calling for a rethinking of our attitudes towards the Russians and communists in general?

I suppose you could look at it that way, I respond.

Well, how else would you look at it, he says in a manner that is more of a declaration than a question.

I am left to ponder the implications.

Here, let me summarize a few parts of the president's speech, JJ declares.

He claims that people have been indoctrinated to believe that peace is impossible.

Well, we always seem to be living under the cloud of nuclear war, I interject.

And why is that? JJ responds. Am I wrong? Is it not the Soviets who are trying to undermine our system, planting spies among us and our allies?

No more than what we are doing, I suppose.

JJ shakes his head in disgust.

Our efforts are minuscule compared to those of our enemies.

What about all those countries that have been subjugated since the end of the war? Poland, East Germany, Estonia, Lithuania, Czechoslovakia, Hungary....

Do you remember what happened when the Hungarians tried to establish themselves as a free country?

I can only nod my head in agreement as he rails on.

Crushed them brutally.

That is the face of an enemy that will stop at nothing to enslave the entire world.

It will build walls to divide countrymen from one another.

And how does our president respond? JJ continues rhetorically.

He picks up a copy of one of the papers.

Here, let me read part of it, this is good:

"Our problems are man-made — therefore, they can be solved by man....

JJ skips to another passage.

"Every graduate of this school, every thoughtful citizen who despairs of war and wishes to bring peace, should begin by looking inward — by examining his own attitude toward the possibilities of peace, toward the Soviet Union, toward the course of the Cold War and toward freedom and peace here at home."

It's incredible. How can he be making these statements? What does he expect to happen, that the Russians will see the error of their ways when we extend an olive branch?

At this point, there is no stopping him.

Listen to this: He says we might find communism, and I quote him here: "Profoundly repugnant…but no government or social system is so evil that its people must be considered as lacking in virtue."

Well, I finally respond, it's an interesting observation.

Interesting! I wonder what the families of the millions of Russians that Stalin ruthlessly slaughtered to maintain his iron grip might think about that. Or, all of those countrymen who have been locked up in prisons in Siberia and the like….

I question, he continues, whether they would think it unfair of us to consider their oppressors to be lacking in virtue.

I interject that the president was speaking about the Russian people, not their system of government.

He pauses to regroup and light another cigarette.

Our president seems to be embarking on a new mission. There's no more — what did he say in his inaugural speech…

He reaches for a file at the corner of his desk.

…I have it here.

He begins to read from the document: "Let the word go forth, to friend and foe alike, that the torch has been passed to a new generation of Americans, tempered by war and unwilling to witness or permit the slow undoing of those human rights to which this nation has always been committed and to which we are committed today at home and around the world."

JJ looks up at me and drags deeply on the cigarette.

That was a strong message he sent just two years ago, and now he's saying what? That he was wrong? What happened to change his mind? It can't be the building of that damnable wall in Berlin or the attempt to put missiles in Cuba to threaten our children as well as the nation as a whole.

I am stunned by both the fury of his remarks and, admittedly, by the seeming contradictions in the president's rhetoric from his inaugural speech to today.

JJ picks up a copy of another one of the newspapers and waves it at me and then puts it down with an air of exhaustion.

Either this president doesn't seem to learn from his mistakes, be it back-channel diplomacy or failure to confront the enemy with force when called upon or....

The thought is left hanging.

What's the military's take on this? I quickly interject in an attempt to keep him from going farther down a path he seems so determined to follow.

I've already talked on the telephone late last night with several of the Joint Chiefs.

Oh, really? Directly?

No, no, no. Members of their staff.

His anger is building to the point that he gets out of his chair, which is quite unusual, and begins pacing the floor.

Given the situation, I decided that it is best to fess up.

I was there, I tell him.

What, he thunders, then sits down and lights yet another cigarette.

How come I didn't know you were going?

I heard about it the other day.

And?

When I looked for you to ask you whether you wanted me to attend, I was told you were lunching at the Rive Gauche…With Cord Meyer…among others.

So?

Well, you didn't return in the afternoon, so I took it upon myself to attend. It was rather interesting.

Okay, okay, JJ responds impatiently. Give me all the details. Spare nothing.

Well, I begin, the stage was wrapped in red, white, and blue bunting, very presidential….

Not that stuff, JJ sighs in disgust. The details of the speech...how was it received?

Well, the audience mostly consisted of students — although I did see several of my confreres from the FBI and the Pentagon at it. Overall, the audience appeared to be receptive, but it's hard to say given the circumstances of last fall. In essence, the president seems to be challenging us to rethink our attitudes about peace and communism.

That's what I gather from the press reports, he interjects.

Oh, I add, he did have a rather interesting comment about breaking free of the cold grip of the military.

JJ cocks his head and drags on his cigarette.

As you have already noted, there was a passage to the effect that because our problems are man-made, we need to solve them.

Hmmh! JJ snorts, then stubs out his cigarette and reaches for a file, signaling the end of our conversation.

Upon leaving, it dawns on me that the president's inaugural speech also contained olive branches of a sort, with many references to a willingness to engage in negotiations to lessen the prospect of war, particularly nuclear engagement. But JJ has pushed aside these contradictions. In his mind, tempered by his experiences, there are no gray areas when it comes to national defense and the need for freedom and liberty to prevail on a global scale.

Just when I thought that the summer doldrums would set in and the heat, humidity, and tendency of elected officials to return to their home bases would slow the pace of activity to a crawl in Washington, the case of John Profumo returns to the forefront and with it a seemingly disproportionate interest here in Langley, the FBI and even the executive branch about a political scandal in the United Kingdom.

John Profumo is secretary of state for war in Harold Macmillan's Conservative government, having held the post of brigadier general during the Second World War before retiring to politics. He is married to Valerie Hobson, a prominent English actress who has just finished an engagement in the lead role in the popular play *The King and I*.

Nonetheless, it became known earlier in March that, for a short period of time in 1961, he had been involved with a certain Christine Keeler, who is said, for British public consumption, to be a model but, in fact, is little more than a prostitute.

For much of the past two years, JJ tells me, the affair had been kept under wraps even though it had been learned that Keeler, at the time of her liaison with Profumo, was simultaneously entertaining the affections of Yevgeny Ivanov, the senior naval attache at the Soviet embassy. Again, another questionable connection with Harold Macmillan, just as was the case with Kim Philby, JJ reminds me.

However, this past March, a Labour MP broke with the British tradition of respecting fellow politician's private lives and made public details about Profumo's relationship with Keeler.

Profumo immediately acknowledged that, indeed, he was acquainted with Keeler but denied that there were any improprieties involved. Nonetheless, Fleet Street, home to much of the British press, has been in a tizzy over the revelation, and stories continued to appear about Keeler, eventually forcing Profumo to own up to his indiscretions, which, it was learned, may have involved four other prostitutes including a Chinese woman, Suzy Chang, and a bleached-blond Czech, Maria Novotny.

At that point, the interest here became more than merely academic. In the course of transcribing tapes from Mary Meyer's Georgetown townhouse, I listen to a conversation between her and sister, Tony, about the president's fascination with the case. Apparently, Ben Bradlee has told his wife that JFK is absorbed by the scandal to the point that the State Department has been directed to forward copies of all correspondence on the matter from David Bruce, the American ambassador to Great Britain.

When I report this to JJ, he tells me that Hoover is also greatly interested in the case and has instructed Charles Bates, the FBI's legal attache in London, to stay on top of it.

It appears that the timing of the disclosures, coming simultaneously with the president's remarks at the American University, have the watchers in a frenetic state.

Even our director, John McCone, who usually shies away from matters such as these, feels that it cannot be ignored and directs Cleveland Cram, deputy chief of station in London, to give the matter his utmost attention. Given that Cram and Bates meet regularly, it's understood that the two will compare notes.

Why all the interest in Profumo here, even though there is a Soviet connection? I ask JJ in a moment of naivety.

JJ rolls his eyes in disbelief but humors me.

Two of these girls have connections to the president, he tells me, matter-of-factly.

They both worked out of New York and have been linked to the president, including one liaison just before the inauguration when Novotny, along with another prostitute, was recruited by Peter Lawford to engage in group sex with the president.

One of them pretended to be a nurse, the other a doctor, JJ continues. The president, of course, was the patient.

It's also known, he continues, that JFK took Chang to dinner at the 21 Club in New York before becoming the president.

My wide-open mouth leads JJ to continue.

There has been speculation that Yevgeny Ivanov, the other man in the affair, may have been coaching these girls to elicit information from Profumo, he tells me.

But the Kennedy's liaisons appear to have been before he took office as president, I point out.

JJ nods in agreement.

The encounters we know about, yes. But despite the information we have been gathering about this president, it's clear that we don't know all the details.

And that worries you, I interject.

Oh, it worries me greatly, he continues. The more I know about this president, the less I suspect that I know. If his personal behavior is of any indication, it's clear he likes to live on the edge, and I don't think that would preclude playing games with the Russians, do you?

I raise my hands in a gesture of surrender and stifle any type of response.

In the midst of all this, the president flies off to Europe for visits to Ireland, England, Germany, and Italy.

First on his itinerary is an official visit to Bonn and then an inspection of the Berlin Wall. In a manner that continues to confound those of us watching his every movement in the shadows, the president appears to have reverted to his Cold War Warrior persona.

To the adoration of Germans attempting to live with the wall, yet another restriction of their freedom, he proclaims himself to be a Berliner and says to thunderous applause: "There are many people in the world who really don't understand, or say they don't, what is the great issue between the free world and the communist world. Let them come to Berlin. There are some who say that communism is the wave of the future. Let them come to Berlin. And there are some who say in Europe and elsewhere, we can work with the communists. Let them come to Berlin. And there are even a few who say that it is true that communism is an evil system, but it permits us to make economic progress. Lass' sie nach Berlin kommen. Let them come to Berlin."

This seeming contradiction of his remarks earlier this month at the American University only serves to stir the pot for JJ and others.

As well, there are considerable murmurs at official levels about the president's choice of traveling companions. It's well known that the "first lady" is expecting again and shouldn't be saddled with the task of accompanying the president abroad, but why does he feel the need to have a female companion with him? Although it is his sister-in-law, Jackie's younger sister Princess Lee Radziwill, her marriage to the Polish Prince, 'Stas' Radziwill, is considered to be on the rocks. There is a definite sense of impropriety to it all, particularly when one knows that the president's recklessness, in terms of women, knows no bounds.

After Germany, it is on to more adulation in Ireland and a brief visit to London to visit with besieged British Prime Minister Harold Macmillan.

Meanwhile, yet another storm erupts here at home when the *New York Journal-American* breaks from its usually slavish support of the president and the Kennedy family to report that "a man who holds a 'very high' elective office" in the administration is linked to what it calls "a Chinese girl" in the Profumo scandal.

For those of us in the know, it can only refer to one person — the president — as the story by James D. Horan and Dom Frasca quotes Maria Novotny as confirming that the woman involved, Suzy Chang, was the "former paramour of the American government official."

Apparently, JJ tells me several days later, Bobby went ballistic when the story appeared, telephoning trusted Washington correspondents to check with their sources to determine the identity of the senior official. One reporter — could it be Hugh Sidey of *Time* magazine, who has an up-and-down relationship with the White House, having provided some salacious remarks about the president's mother to advertisers — is interrupted by the attorney general several times in the course of trying to host a Saturday afternoon barbecue.

Not satisfied with the results, the AG eventually calls the pair of reporters onto the carpet and demands to know the identity of the official.

At first, the two demur, but eventually, they confirm that it is, indeed, the president.

To make matters worse, the conversation is witnessed by Courtney Evans, the FBI liaison officer to the attorney general's office, who undoubtedly passes the information on to Hoover.

What was Bobby thinking, having Evans present? I ask JJ, who admits to being similarly confused.

It beats me, he says, adding that when the AG later questioned Evans as to whether the information had been passed on to Hoover, the official confirmed it.

Do you think the attorney general is becoming overwhelmed with the duplicity of his brother? I venture.

He's certainly exhibiting signs of stress, JJ acknowledges. This questioning of the reporters served no useful purpose. In fact, it gives credibility to the story. And having Evans sitting in only makes it worse because now we all know.

I don't know how they can go about normal business with these distractions, I conclude.

JJ just nods in agreement.

There is a frenetic quality in and around JJ's office. People are constantly coming and going in an unlikely manner since the breaking of a story by Clark Mollenhoff in the *Des Moines Register*. Mollenhoff is a highly regarded national reporter despite representing a smaller regional newspaper.

By all standards, this piece is even more volatile than the report this past spring by the Hearst reporters when the Profumo scandal was at its most incendiary point.

Mollenhoff's scoop reports that the Senate Rules Committee is planning to hear testimony about an Ellen Rometsch and her abrupt expulsion in late summer from the U.S. It also states that the committee was in the process of examining various allegations regarding Senate employees as well as Senate members.

However, the biggest bombshell is reserved for a paragraph that states: The FBI had "established that the beautiful brunette had been attending parties with congressional leaders and some prominent New Frontiersmen from the executive branch of government..."

Does Mollenhoff know that the president is involved? JJ wonders aloud. Certainly, the two guys from the *New York World* knew that JFK had been involved with some of the Profumo girls back before he took office.

Well, they never named the president in their story, so I suppose the same is true of Mollenhoff, I venture.

I don't quite understand that, JJ says in an unusually puzzled manner.

Why don't these reporters publish all of their information?

Fear of being sued? I respond.

No, that can't be the case. Certainly, the Kennedy family has the Hearsts in their pocket. So why even publish a story that's bound to raise suspicions, particularly if that is going to endanger your relationship with the president?

I have to confess my lack of knowledge regarding newspaper practices and ethics.

JJ stews over it for a while, but eventually, we move on.

So, where is Mollenhoff getting his information from? I wonder aloud.

Oh, unquestionably Senator John Williams, JJ responds with authority, thankful for being back on firmer ground. Did you see these sections? He says, picking up a copy of the article and referring to various paragraphs that have been highlighted.

It reports that she was born in East Germany and still has relatives on the other side of the Iron Curtain.

I nod in agreement.

And, JJ continues, the story states: "The possibility that her activity might be connected with espionage was of some concern to security investigators because of the high rank of her male companions. Last summer, the FBI started an investigation of the girl. With less than a week's notice, she and her husband were sent back to Germany…at the request of the State Department."

Did you have any involvement in that? I ask him directly.

He frowns and shakes his head. Involvement in sending her back to Germany?

No, I respond, in the story.

You know I don't leak information to the press.

No, not directly, I concur, but I find it interesting that Mollenhoff also reported extensively on the decision by the administration last year to suddenly drop Boeing from the TFX contract and award it to General Dynamics.

Well, that could have been the FBI, JJ quickly replies. After all, they were the ones that told you about General Dynamics having the goods on the president and using it to their benefit. You know, it wouldn't surprise me that Hoover gave Senator Williams or Mollenhoff the dope on the lovely Miss Rometsch.

Really?

Oh, yes. It would be Hoover's way of sending a message to the president. Sort of a tip of the iceberg kind of thing. You know, he'd been sending memos to Bobby about her without getting any results, so…failing that, a word or two to a favorite, a peak at a file or two, well…. JJ lets the thought drift away.

In the wake of the Mollenhoff piece, reports are rampant that the attorney general is putting pressure on Hoover to help keep the Remetsch affair from becoming even more public.

Nonetheless, ever since the Bobby Baker scandal broke, there has been a growing sense that it will envelop the White House.

JJ asks me to snoop around to see what I can find out. Among the suggestions is that we bug the townhouse of Baker's secretary, Nancy Carole Tyler, which she shares with a secretary to Florida Senator George Smathers, a Mary Jo Kopechne.

Aside from the fact that Tyler is extremely attractive, she has been linked romantically with Baker. Interestingly, she is listed as a cousin on documents relating to the home, apparently to satisfy occupancy requirements which require that owner occupants be relatives.

Nevertheless, I question the usefulness of putting a bug there since Kopechne, a former teacher, is not known to be much of a partier, which would limit its usefulness. But JJ is adamant, stressing that Baker uses the home to entertain political and business associates. He thinks we might turn up more information regarding the various liaisons involving Ellen Rometsch.

Unfortunately, aside from some additional incriminating evidence regarding Tyler and Baker, the bugs serve little purpose other than to confirm that we are not the only ones with an interest in the home of Misses Tyler and Kopechne. Our operation team, which was involved in wiring the house, reported the discovery of other listening devices.

Are they FBI or foreign? JJ asks when I pass on this piece of information. They appear to be domestic, I tell him, but that doesn't necessarily rule out the possibility of them being planted by the Russians.

Do you know whether Rometsch was ever present in the home? JJ continues.

It doesn't appear so, I tell him. All of the available information suggests that most of her activity involved liaisons at Quorum Club, a private hideaway at the Carroll Arms Hotel adjacent to a Senate office building operated by Baker, or visits to the White House.

Visits to the White House, JJ thunders.

Yes, Bill Thompson....

The president's friend?

Yes, he had her brought to his apartment and then took her to the White House....

The White House? JJ repeats in disbelief.

On more than one occasion. Apparently, she looks like Elizabeth Tayler.

That piques his interest even more.

Really.

And she is most accommodating, I tell him. Baker claims that everyone who hooked up with her had a very enjoyable time. The president, in particular, said it was the best time he had ever had in his life.

She'll surely be missed.

By everyone, JJ says with a forced smile. Everyone.

JJ says he doesn't know how Bobby managed to do it, but somehow, he has convinced Hoover to block any attempts to have Rometsch return from Germany and testify before the Senate. While working together in the office, JJ takes a call from one of his FBI contacts, who tells him that Courtney Evans, the FBI liaison officer to the attorney general, has been summoned to see the AG and told to give Hoover the message that great possible harm might come to the nation if the Senate is allowed to instigate irresponsible action of a partisan nature through hearings on the Rometsch allegations.

JJ shakes his head in amazement while repeating the gist of the conversation to me.

Apparently, he says, the president didn't know the background of this Rometsch woman before getting involved.

Oh, I respond. What is her background?

JJ drags on yet another Virginia Slim while pondering the new revelations.

Well, we knew she was born in East Germany and that she had been a member of the communist party….

It's another unusual connection to the Soviets and their allies, he continues, then stops abruptly before continuing. You know, it's not the first time our president has been involved with women with links to a potential enemy.

What?

Back in the Forties, during the war, our president got involved with a Danish journalist, Ingrid Marie…ah Arvid.

So?

Well, she had a connection to Hitler. Something to do with the '36 Olympics.

Oh, so she must have been a bit older than Kennedy.

Yea, she'd been around the block more than a few times and was in the process of getting divorced from her Hungarian husband. Anyways, your boy couldn't get enough of her to the point that he was moved out of Washington, where he was serving in a military function, and transferred to South Carolina.

Nonetheless, the liaisons continued, and apparently, Hoover started wiretapping Kennedy's apartment.

JJ lets that thought drift away as he drags on yet another smoke.

You don't think this current contretemps is anything more than the president's insatiable need for variety in women? I ask. You know our Secret Service friends have overheard him on more than one occasion complain that he gets a migraine if he doesn't "get a strange piece of ass every day."

JJ just shakes his head and picks up the thread of conversation relating to the telephone conversation with the FBI agent.

Evans even called the president, who said he was considering calling Senate Majority Leader Mike Mansfield and Minority Leader Everett Dirksen to ask them to meet with Hoover.

And have they? I ask.

Don't know. It probably wasn't necessary because Hoover will add this to the lengthening laundry list that he holds over the president's head. You know, it probably kills the president that he has to try and shut down this Senate committee in order to protect his butt.

Huh?

There's more to this Baker thing than just the women, and the president isn't the only senior official in his administration who could come under close scrutiny.

By now, my curiosity is piqued, and JJ continues.

Baker is a protégé of LBJ. He's got financial ties to some vending machine company that has been awarded several federal contracts even though the company is not up and operating yet.

That's interesting, I respond, but other than his earlier connections, how does that hurt the vice president?

You're right; there might have only been a little bit of heat on the V.P., which would eventually blow away.

I nod my head.

What's more problematic for Johnson, however, are some complaints that he's using his office and personal standing to enhance his business interests in Texas, particularly his Austin TV and radio stations.

I start to laugh, and JJ joins in.

You know LBJ is always desperately looking to make a buck. It's all about his daddy going bankrupt and losing his political standing and respect in the Texas legislature.

Regardless, apparently, he bought some life insurance recently from a broker in Maryland, and as part of the deal, LBJ forced the agent to buy advertising on his Texas stations…and…

JJ starts to chuckle again.

…Even cajoled him into giving him a television set and a new stereo as the price of doing business.

I've heard that LBJ can be a very persuasive man when he sets his mind to it, I add.

But why would the president be upset about this information not being made public? I would think that he wouldn't want any negative publicity about a member of his administration.

JJ looks at me in amazement.

The last thing the president wants is LBJ on the ticket in 1964. He never wanted him as his Veep in the first place. Only accepted him to avoid a mess at the convention. If it came out in a public forum that LBJ was using his office for personal gain, then the president could use that information as a pretext to dump him.

Couldn't he do that anyway, without these revelations?

Not that easily with the vice president, JJ allows. LBJ simply has too many friends in both the House and the Senate who the president is beholden to.

But the bottom line is that the president wants to be rid of LBJ so that he can clear the way for Bobby to run for president in 1968.

And, he continues after a brief silence, we simply can't have that happen.

After several days of waiting to see how the situation plays out, we hear that Hoover has let the president off the hook. Understandably, JJ is furious. Apparently, Hoover not only met with the attorney general and assured him that Rometsch wouldn't get a visa and, therefore, wouldn't be available to testify but also agreed to talk to both Mansfield and Dirksen in an effort to keep the Senate hounds at bay.

I have several other issues that I need to speak with JJ about, but he tells me to put them on hold because he has more pressing concerns to deal with.

Oh, more Golitsyn? I ask.

No, no, he responds vacantly. Clearly, he is absorbed with something else.

After what seems like a painfully long stretch of silence, he begins slowly and deliberately.

There is no question that our president is a duplicitous individual in both his personal and public lives, JJ declares.

The question is the extent to which his duplicitous behavior extends....

In his personal life?

No, I could care less about that, although it is important when viewed in the context of his overall behavior. He pauses.

I just don't know, he finally exclaims, shaking his head vigorously.

I just don't know.

I stare intently, fearful of what next will emerge.

Again, he repeats his fear of the unknown.

Is it just that he has always been this way and that the defects of his character have become magnified by his ascent in responsibility?

I stare at him.

He looks down and fiddles with some papers.

This is my concern, he finally speaks. Am I allowing my personal distaste for this individual to color my perception? Or....

It seems to hang in the balance.

Or are the danger signs too clear to be ignored?

Oh, my, I couldn't possibly, I pause, staring at him wide-eyed...make that kind of determination.

It draws JJ up abruptly.

No one...no one in their right mind, or, at least, no normal person would want to draw that kind of conclusion, he allows.

But?

My responsibilities ensure that I cannot enjoy the life of a normal person.

You must be distrustful?

Not just distrustful!

Skeptical?

It's not that either. I just can't....

His face distorts in a manner I have never witnessed.

I can't accept anything at face value, he finally declares.

I have to be constantly questioning: What do I think I know? What do I know to be true?

He pauses for more than just a moment.

And, of even greater importance: What don't I know?

It's that last question that hangs over us, particularly myself.

With that declaration, he appears to be visibly shrinking, shriveling up in his chair, sliding down below his files, a fume of smoke suggesting that he has imploded.

I quietly exit his office.

JJ summons me to his suite, and we proceed directly into its deepest reaches, but not before we go through a complex series of locks and checks.

It's been some time since I have been inside his inner sanctum, and I am amazed at the transformation. Each of the four walls has been stripped of any previous decoration, and in its place is a series of charts, laboriously prepared in chronological order based on what appears to be bristol board or some form of heavier material. Along the floor of each wall is a series of bankers' boxes containing files relating to the activities outlined on each wall.

Each file is color-coded, containing a numerical designation. On the first wall, to the left of the door, coded blue, is the president's sexual history, such as we know it, detailing every indiscretion to date, both before and during his administration.

The second, facing more directly, coded yellow, is devoted to political developments during the past three years and appears to contain the most entries.

The third, green, lists people who have been bought and sold in the process.

On the final wall, to the right of the door, are two complex, family-tree-style outlines of agents and their relationships. The first, coded red, is the busiest of the two detailing Soviet agents around the world, including North America, while the second, coded black, is a single entry devoted exclusively to the president.

In the middle of the room is a simple, oblong table of about eight feet in length and four feet in width, not unlike the kind that might be used at banquet functions. On each side of the table is a secretarial-style chair without arm supports but on wheels, which I suspect enables its occupant, presumably JJ, to move up and down the length of the table when reviewing files without having to stand up and down constantly.

JJ sits in one of them and allows me to peruse the room. After a brief inspection, he directs me to sit in the other vacant chair with my back to the door.

We have a great deal to talk about, he tells me, matter-of-factly, stopping momentarily to take a sip of the proverbial mug which is constantly at his side these days, minus any appearance of coffee, which is easily identifiable because he likes his with lots of cream. This beverage is more the smokey amber color commonly associated with whisky, preferably bourbon.

You remember Dr. Max Jacobson?

Dr. Feel-Good, I respond.

Correct, JJ acknowledges, then sips somewhat absent-mindedly from the mug before continuing.

The doctor, I am told, has been even more active than usual of late.

Oh, really, I say with feigned interest.

However, with no further response coming from JJ, I get up and start walking around the room, stopping at each wall to read bits and pieces from each one. I know most of them from my own first-hand reports to JJ, but there are some items that surprise me.

JJ watches warily, constantly sipping from his mug.

I notice that the room its remarkably absent of cigarette smoke and that there are no ashtrays filled to the brim and overflowing as is his trademark.

Are you trying to quit? I ask him.

Quit, quit what?

Cigarettes.

He chuckles sheepishly.

They're not allowed in here. Too dangerous.

Oh, for sure, this room is dangerous, but not because of cigarettes.

He mumbles what appears to be some form of agreement.

So, what does this all add up to? I finally ask him.

I think it's very obvious, don't you?

I grimace while mentally composing my response.

Is it not possible, I finally allow, that we simply have a president who is the sum of all our worst sins?

Go on.

He's a philanderer, no doubt. I am sure there are medical people whose diagnosis would be that he is, first and foremost, a sex addict or, worse still, suffering from some other mental defect.

Oh, probably, JJ allows. He's probably also dependent upon a variety of drugs.

You mean the LSD and weed that Mary Meyer has been supplying him with?

No, I'm talking about the drugs being supplied by his so-called physician.

Then there's the bribes he and his family paid out to steal the election.

I nod in agreement.

The bribes he's been paid to further the interests of others, such as the California businessman that Judith Exner Campbell dealt with.

He pauses for a moment to sip from his mug.

Blackmail? I exclaim.

Right! You've only seen the slimy dealings like the THX project where the president appears to have willfully directed our armed forces to buy and use an inferior product just to protect his ass...or, should I say, his fondness for ass.

The explosive nature of his comment startles me.

Is there more? Has Golitsyn told you? I hesitate, fearful of what I am thinking of asking....

JJ just stares for a moment before responding.

Has he told me...told me what?

Before I know it, I am blurting out my worst fears. Has he told you he's an agent?

Who? Golitsyn? JJ responds, almost playfully.

No, you know who I mean.

JJ just stares back at me.

You won't say, or can't say?

Again, he sips from his mug, then after some contemplation, changes the subject.

What about his dealings with the military? The Cuban stuff?

It's very disturbing, I agree.

Disturbing?

More than that, I suppose.

JJ gets out of his chair and strides around the room in a robust manner I have not witnessed of late.

This president committed nothing short of murder when he left those boys on the beach at the Bay of Pigs without the benefit of that second air strike that he had promised.

It was a political decision, we discussed this before.

A political decision?

Okay, a military decision. The kind of sacrifice that military men make when they send soldiers to fight battles that they know they can't win.

JJ just looks at me with disgust.

I don't know what kind of officers you served under, but they certainly wouldn't have been American. We don't put our boys in harm's way unless we're committed to doing everything we can to succeed. Now, the Russians? That's a different story. They don't value human life like we do.

I am shaken by the vehemence of his remarks.

JJ sits down, as much to cool off as to catch his breath

Alright, I agree. We have a…

I hesitate to find the appropriate description.

…a corrupt president, morally corrupt. One whose motives, at the least, are questionable. Someone that we're not sure that we could count on to protect the best interests of this country when the chips are down. I could go on. It's quite an indictment.

Oh, you got that right, JJ allows.

But, and I pause momentarily, don't we have the means to deal with this in an election?

JJ begins to laugh, almost giddily, but it quickly dissolves into angry silence.

I get up and wave my hand in a sweeping motion around the room. I mean, look at all the intel that you have collected. I'm sure if just half of this became public during the campaign next year or the period leading up to it, the president would be defeated.

You'd think so, wouldn't you? JJ allows.

I rise to the bait.

Definitely!

JJ just smiles.

Politics, he says with a shake of his head, it's not the surest thing. Who knows what might happen? People have been fooled before, and I suspect they'll be fooled again.

Maybe you don't have enough faith in the American people, I hear myself declare. Starting with the Founding Fathers, generations of Americans have proven themselves. Our systems and beliefs, they're all based on change by democratic means. Isn't that what we are here to protect?

Of course, he responds condescendingly, we are a model for the entire world...

But... He lets that hang in mid-air for what seems like an eternity before continuing

...I think it's fair to say that we've never, in our long and glorious history, had to deal with the prospect that our president is a traitor. That raises the issue beyond allowing the people to decide in fifteen months' time, wouldn't you agree?

My stunned expression says more than I want to.

I am sure we'll have more time to explore this in the next month or so, he says as his way of dismissing me.

Nonetheless, I am not quite ready to throw in the towel.

Okay, that's all very likely, but...

You're right to hesitate, JJ allows in an unusually conciliatory manner, in some respects, all of that is just typical political shortcomings. I could name you any number of politicians who fall into one or another of those categories.

I'm sure you could, I hear myself concurring.

But....

There's a but I declare.

Oh, yes, a big but....

He pauses to gather himself, cleans his glasses, reaches for the crumpled pack of Virginia Slims, and then hurriedly puts them back in his pocket.

But?

You know there's far more to this than just the peccadillos of this man, many though they may be.

I am left to reflect on the seriousness of the unmentioned accusations.

JJ moves towards the door, a signal that we are done for the moment.

One of the key issues that JJ has not spoken much about lately but is constantly on his mind is the president's determination to get the Soviets to agree to a non-proliferation pact. Interestingly, negotiations picked up considerably last fall after the Cuban standoff when Nikita Khrushchev sent a letter to the president, dated October 30, just days after the crisis appeared to be averted. In the letter, he outlines a range of bold initiatives ostensibly to avoid the on-and-off negotiations during the past year, with the key sticking points being the question of how many 'black boxes' (automated test-detection stations) would be put in place and the number of on-site inspections that would be allowed. Initially, we were seeking anywhere between 10-20 stations, whereas the Russians wanted only three. During the course of negotiations, we had consistently reduced our demands, first to twelve, then to seven, then six, but none satisfied the Soviet leader, who subsequently withdrew his offer of three.

Although not within his daily scope of operations, JJ has been following developments with typically keen interest and sees the president's negotiation strategy of dropping our demands as yet another sign of his weakness in dealing with Russia and stoking further conspiracy fears. The involvement in the negotiations of the Macmillan government in England only heightens JJ's concerns, given his disdain for the British Prime Minister.

Since July, negotiations in Moscow have often included Khrushchev, whose main sticking point is that the Anglo-American inspection plan would amount to espionage — an opinion that on more than one occasion has elicited hearty guffaws from an otherwise reticent JJ.

Nonetheless, within ten days, an agreement is reached, the speed of which both astonishes and worries JJ.

The following day, the president makes a 26-minute televised national address in which he states that since the development of nuclear weapons, "all mankind has been struggling to escape from the darkening prospect of mass destruction on earth."

Interestingly, Khrushchev's remarks, following those of the president, are less optimistic, declaring that the treaty will not end the arms race and by itself would not "avert the danger of war."

For JJ, Khrushchev's statement raises many flags of concern. Nonetheless, he appears to be focused on other issues, including the increased involvement of the U.S. in the growing Vietnam conflict.

There are rumors that in addition to his ongoing practices, he has initiated increased wiretapping of U.S. dissidents to America's growing involvement in this far-away war. To make matters worse, there is increased chatter amongst ourselves and the military about the need to remove South Vietnamese

President Ngo Dinh Diem by whatever means necessary, foreshadowing future events.

For some time, JJ had been trying to arrange a luncheon with Allen, even though he is now retired. It includes some of Dulles' former lieutenants who are still active in the company.

Unlike previous meals at the usual places, JJ is determined that the location of this one remains a secret until the last minute.

Dulles is amused by it all but agrees to what he considers to be unnecessary cloak-and-dagger precautions.

The plan is to have JJ book suitable transportation to pick up the various members of the party and bring them to the location. All goes according to plan, and we arrive at a restaurant on the outskirts of Washington in Virginia, where we are taken to a private room with its own bar and served steaks, which had been pre-ordered by JJ based on previous personal preferences.

Dulles, of course, wants to be brought up to date on all of the minutiae that he no longer hears, and the meal is filled with small talk and the usual company gossip.

JJ appears moody and withdrawn, ignoring even the lightest banter while quickly downing several martinis in quick succession. Eventually, the conversation simply dries up as everyone concentrates on finishing their meal. But JJ merely toys with his steak to the point that it becomes so noticeable that Dulles confronts him.

What's the problem, Jim, don't like the steak? The company? This is your party!

JJ squirms, but Dulles persists. Okay, what's eating you, Jim?

JJ stands up and walks to the door and locks it.

Everyone is watching.

Allen, how do we deal with a president who seems to be intent on misleading us on every occasion, much less the American public?

You could hear the proverbial pin drop.

So much for social, small talk, Dulles drolly responds.

JJ just shakes his head and plunges onward.

The Missile Gap he trumpeted in the 1960 campaign did not exist; that was disinformation in its finest form designed to make his candidacy something that it wasn't. Who would suspect an individual who pretends to be the exact opposite? Champion of freedom, tempered by war, you know, the stuff from his inauguration. Meanwhile, an administration under an experienced vice president with a proven record of anti-communism is consigned to the dustbin.

There is no response, but everyone has stopped eating.

JJ hurtles on.

Kennedy even managed to make Nixon look soft on communism. It was beautiful, just like Hoover railing about faggots. And it didn't matter that Ike took him aside on the eve of his inauguration and pointed out to him that we still had a considerable strategic edge over the Russians in part because of nuclear-equipped subs patrolling the coasts of the Soviet Union.

Alright, Jim, that's enough, Dulles interjects.

But, Allen, we can't ignore what happened at the Bay of Pigs.

Helms jumps in.

So, what about last year? As much as we might not like the man or his brother, they faced down the Russians over missiles in Cuba?

JJ smiles.

Another example of disinformation at its finest. Is it not possible that the whole event was contrived to make our president appear to be something he really isn't?

A murmur of protestation starts to build but is waved off by JJ.

Hold on, he demands, staring down the room. How else do you explain the interpretation of all the confusing official messages unless you understand and recognize that the president and his brother were working from a different set of information than everyone else?

Besides, we end up removing missiles from Turkey, much to the Russians' satisfaction. In fact, much to Khrushchev's satisfaction. . . .

Dulles chuckles, and the tension dissipates momentarily.

You may have a point there, Jim, but it did rob Khrushchev of one of his favorite little grandstanding performances.

And how is that, Allen?

Dulles pauses to light his pipe, then continues.

I'd be surprised if you hadn't heard, but it's common knowledge that, on occasions, when entertaining guests at his summer home in Soviet Georgia, the esteemed Soviet leader likes to direct the attention of his guests across the Black Sea towards Turkey and declare: Those are U.S. missiles over there, aimed at my dacha.

Everyone laughs, but not JJ, who plows on and is determined not to be derailed by amusing anecdotes.

Do any of you think that if, and I emphasize if, the president of the United States of America was really determined to get rid of Castro, the bastard still would be strutting about his little island kingdom threatening us and our Latin American allies?

Besides, the president seemed intent on ignoring the prospect that the Russians were putting missiles on the island until he was confronted with incontrovertible proof by our people that they existed. Then, he had no option but to talk a good fight....

That alerts Helms.

Look, it turns out that I had a meeting with Bobby moments after the president had briefed him about the situation in Cuba and the discovery of the missiles, and he was in a state of shock.

He just kept repeating: "Dick, is it true? Dick, is it true?"

JJ remains nonplussed.

Let me ask you something, Richard?

Helms looks at JJ warily.

Why was such a big deal being made about missiles in Cuba when the Soviets had subs on constant patrol just miles outside of our boundaries in international water that could deliver the same warheads with the same results?

Helms glares at JJ.

After all, we have 3,000 warheads and nearly 300 missile launchers, and according to even our most liberal estimates, the Soviet Union only has about 250 warheads and maybe, just maybe, 40 launchers. Do you think the balance is changed by dropping a couple into Cuba?

Dulles puts his pipe down.

So, what are you saying, Jim?

I think the whole Cuba thing was drummed up to make Kennedy look like a hero, particularly in the wake of the disasters in Vienna and Berlin, where, by all accounts, Khrushchev made mincemeat out of a young, inexperienced president. Now, he looks strong and resolute and in no danger of being turfed out of office in Sixty-Four. You know, the Russians must be shitting their pants thinking about the alternative to Kennedy.

Goldwater? Someone calls out.

Not just Barry but all of the others that his administration would bring to the table.

And here's something else to think about…and by the way, this info is available to all of us, but no one seems to have tied it together.

Helms gives a sarcastic snort.

But you're going to tell us.

Damn right, I am, Richard.

He pauses to ensure that we are focused on what he has to say.

During this so-called Cuban crisis, we were at our highest military alert — just short of all-out war. We had more paratroopers ready to drop on Cuba than we had at Normandy, where we faced a stronger and better-prepared foe. More than 100,000 combat-ready troops were deployed to ports along the East Coast. A huge fleet, including 40,000 Marines, was at sea and at the ready, just moments away from battle stations. A total of 579 fighter jets were ready to fly 1,190 combat sorties in the first twenty-four hours of any confrontation. Preparations were at a fever pitch; we were on a war footing that was unprecedented during a time of peace.

Helms mutters something about circumstances dictating such actions.

JJ shakes his head in disgust.

Then answer me this, Richard: Why weren't the Russians gearing up?

Helms gives him a quizzical look.

Huh?

During all of this saber-rattling on our part, the Russians are merely going about things like it was business as usual.

But they had that convoy steaming towards Cuba, Helms responds.

Freighters.

More than just freighters, he asserts.

Listen, Richard, if the danger existed for all-out war, nuclear war as the White House painted it, the Russians would also have been on full alert. But they weren't. In fact, and you check this out for yourself, Richard, there were no military moves whatsoever.

Their fleet of liquid-fueled ICBM launchers, which require hours of preparation before launching, were never put on alert. Soviet reserve forces were not called up, and there were no military moves in Berlin.

Helms appears to be perplexed as do the rest.

I'm telling you that there never was a threat. It was just…almost like it was stage-managed to make our president look good just before the mid-term elections. In fact, at the height of the crisis, with the Soviet ships steaming towards our naval blockade and all of the nation glued to TV sets, wondering what the hell is going to happen? Will we all be here tomorrow? What do you think the president is doing?

No one responds.

He and Jackie are having dinner with an old acquaintance, Charles Bartlett and his wife — by the way, Bartlett's the man credited with first introducing him to Jackie. It's as if nothing is happening, at least nothing of any consequence sufficient to warrant cancelling a dinner with some old acquaintances.

Dulles smiles. Well, Jim, he chuckles, albeit somewhat nervously now; as always, you are as entertaining as you are informative.

I don't think it's a laughing matter, Allen.

You never do, Jim.

All I am saying is that there certainly is reason to consider the possibility that it may not be what it appears to be.

Dulles smiles at JJ

Okay, Jim, now is this a real concern, or has that third martini unleashed your darkest fears?

You know booze doesn't affect me like that, Allen, JJ replies defensively.

I'm not sure what I know anymore, Jim.

Silence envelopes the room for what seems like an eternity

But now that JJ's on a roll, he's not about to be stopped.

By the way, in the lead-up to all of this, the president and his brother are ratcheting up their so-called back-channel diplomacy with Bolshakov.

Has it ever occurred to anyone that he and his successor Dobrynin, because of their constant contact with the Kennedys, were in a perfect position to be their control?

What! Dulles exclaims.

Allen, Bobby met with Bolshakov six times alone in July of 1962. We have surveillance confirming that information.

Another diner pipes up: We had surveillance on the attorney general of the USA, who also happens to be the brother of the president?

It's not just us, JJ answers. The FBI is watching them like hawks, too.

After allowing that information to sink in, JJ continues.

So, let's take a closer look at this. In the summer of '62, your successor, John McCone — appointed by Kennedy after pushing you out...

Dulles interjects.

Now, let's not get into that again.

JJ persists.

Nonetheless, Allen, the president's own man, is telling him in no uncertain terms that the Soviets have put SAMs in Cuba and that there is the possibility that medium-range ballistic missiles are next.

At some point, I've since learned McCone even recommended the deployment of sufficient forces to occupy Cuba, destroy the regime, free the people, and establish a peaceful regime. What could be better for a president who has been badgering us since he came into office to do something to get rid of Castro?

He's being handed the pretext on a golden platter to accomplish his objective and what does he do?

JJ pauses dramatically.

Nothing. In fact, worse still, in response to public revelations about the Soviet buildup by Keating, a New York senator. He issues a statement saying there is nothing to be concerned about.

Now, how the hell do you square that?

After the Bay of Pigs, the president didn't trust us, Helms answers.

Besides, we fed that info to Keating.

Oh, JJ responds, so the president doesn't trust us? Well, maybe it should be the other way around.

There is a collective gasp, but JJ ignores it.

Later, Bobby starts spreading the news to loyal senators and congressmen that McCone never told them anything. That he is just covering his own butt and that of the agency, it's just politics, according to Bobby. Well, damn it, it's more than just politics, and you know it.

By this point, Dulles has become increasingly agitated.

You realize that this discussion is, at the very least, seditious. If any of it ever leaks out, we can all be charged with treason and, if not executed, locked in prison with the key thrown away.

Allen, don't go soft on me now, JJ exclaims, but Dulles just waves him off.

As interesting as it all is, I cannot be a party to any further discussions of this sort.

With that, Dulles prepares to leave.

I assume I can get a taxi here, Jim?

JJ nods, unlocks the door, and Dulles leaves the room.

JJ surveys the table.

Okay, we've got his blessing, but we're on our own.

His blessing? Helms asks. How did I miss that?

There are various grunts of agreement.

JJ looks at Helms.

You know Allen, he never gives a direct answer. What's more important is that he didn't tell us to cease and desist. He just said he cannot be a party to any more such discussions.

There is a nervous shuffling of dinner utensils.

Finally, Helms gathers himself together and starts to exit the room, mumbling something about catching a ride with Allen.

The rest of the table remains thunderstruck.

JJ continues to ramble on as if nothing has happened.

You know, prior to the Bay of Pigs, we had everything under control. Where have we been since? It's the president who controls our agenda in a way that no other one has, and our record has been pathetic as a result.

He pauses for effect.

I'll admit it, he fooled us. Fooled me, just like...

And he pauses for dramatic effect.

...Philby.

From there, he segues into a disjointed line of thought.

You know, the president inexplicably allowed Khrushchev to hammer him in Vienna, and shortly thereafter, the Berlin Wall goes up. Then, he pretends that his back is bothering him. He has to be lifted from the plane on his arrival home from the summit, what a loser.

Finally, someone else speaks up.

Doesn't it occur to you, Angleton, that this room might be bugged?

JJ waves him off.

No one knew about this location except me, and I personally swept it in advance.

First, one, then another rises and leaves. Finally, there is only JJ and myself remaining.

JJ seems to be oblivious to the fact that he has been deserted.

They'll come around, he tells me. Just wait and see.

A couple of days later Dulles asks me to meet with him.

He wastes little time getting to the point.

I'm worried about Jim, he tells me.

I know he feels like he's under a lot of pressure to make sure that there is not another occurrence like Philby's where our national security is compromised. He pauses to relight his pipe. And I suppose my leaving hasn't helped matters.

For once, my silence doesn't deter him

What can you tell me?

I'm not sure, I respond. There's a lot of information that I am not privy to.

Yes, of course, but....

I can only tell you the barest bones.

There is evidence that has been gathered by people who not only are concerned about some of the developments that JJ mentioned yesterday but who are also appalled by the conduct of the president.

Christ! Dulles exclaims in a totally out-of-character manner.

As long as we've had presidents, there's been a bit of hanky-panky going on.

This is not a bit, Allen, I respond.

Ahhhh, he replies in a tone of resignation.

There is no question, I tell him, that the president's conduct goes well beyond that of a little extra-curricular activity. It's like you said before. He is reckless beyond belief, but it's not just a woman or two; it's prostitutes and.…

What, he exclaims.

There are some suggestions that there is group sex and not just between men and women.

My God!

At the very least, there is growing evidence that if he hasn't already been turned, he is extremely vulnerable.

After a long pause, Dulles mutters something unintelligible.

Better men have come a cropper over less, I remind him.

Dulles just shakes his head wearily.

It's out of control, isn't it?

It's a very dangerous situation and getting worse by the day, I reply.

What can I tell him?

Probably nothing now, I respond. He expects that you understand.

My God, Dulles exclaims a second time. His hands shake, and fresh tobacco spills out of his pipe.

I promise to keep Allen informed, but it's as if he's no longer listening.

November 22, 1963

There is tantamount to panic in the nation's capital. Everywhere one goes, the incessant reports on the radio are heard. Walter Cronkite, the nation's most trusted purveyor of TV news, is on the screen well before his normal appearance time. Solemnly, he reads from copy, newly ripped from the wire machines: "From Dallas, Texas…." At this point, he inadvertently reveals what for most people is a sense of disbelief, "the flash, apparently official," before finishing the words on the page: "President Kennedy died at 1 p.m. Central Standard Time…" slowly he removes his glasses and glances up to his right to what must be an array of clocks, stares vacantly into the camera and replaces his glasses in the process of finishing his most devasting report: "…two p.m. Eastern Standard Time, some thirty-eight minutes ago." Grimacing painfully, he begins to relate what is happening with Vice President Johnson, but at that point, shock obliterates any meaningful recollection or understanding of what is happening.

Later, people will ask each other: Where were you when the president was killed?

For most, the answer will be somewhat mundane and yet a memory that they will carry with them to their grave.

For me, the question quickly becomes: Where was James Jesus Angleton?

He had not been in the office much of late, and on the few occasions that he was there, he was closeted, often in the vault no less, with people that I do not recognize nor have heard of. Some have unmistakable accents.

But these are rare. For the most part, he is simply unavailable. At the time, I had given little thought to it as I had increasingly come to welcome his sojourns away from the office. But now my concerns are heightened.

Once I regain my senses, I immediately try to contact him. Calling Bertha proves fruitless. The shock of the event has penetrated even her iron will and resolve. She blubbers on about staff crying and not knowing what to do or how to reach JJ.

After much contemplation, I decide to call JJ's home number, an action I have never taken before.

But there is no answer.

Failing that, I am left to watch the post-killing coverage alone, including viewing the numerous reruns of the president being shot and the subsequent shooting of the apparent assassin, Lee Harvey Oswald.

Eventually, JJ surfaces.

Naturally, I wondered where he had been, and I began to ask how the events surrounding the death of the president would impact us and our operation.

But he would have nothing to do with my questions.

I started to stutter about not seeing him in the office of late, nor him answering my calls, but he cut me off sharply, shaking his head at the temerity of my questioning.

Your job is not to monitor my activities but rather to carry out the tasks I assign to you. Is that clear?

A staring match ensues as I refuse to acknowledge that directive. Not for the first time, I find myself questioning what we had been doing and what might be the consequences.

I am never, he pauses, gathering himself to his full height of six feet, four inches, away from my responsibilities, regardless of where this position takes me.

I decide on a less confrontational tactic.

Have you been in contact with the president? I inquire.

As a matter of record, I have been. Lyndon reached out to me a day or so after his return to the capital.

Oh?

JJ sits down and starts shuffling some papers.

And....

Well, he wanted my take on the situation

And some assurances, I ask.

Assurances, he thunders.

About our involvement?

Our involvement?

Yes, he didn't ask you whether we knew or expected anything to happen.

He sighs.

Yes, he asked me in a manner that only Lyndon is capable of doing.

And your response?

I told him what he needed and wanted to know!

No one will ever accuse Lyndon Baines Johnson of being a man of inaction, and in the hours and days immediately following the assassination of John F. Kennedy, there is a whirl of activity surrounding the new president.

Within a week, LBJ sets into motion a commission, headed by Chief Justice Earl Warren, former governor of California, to examine and report back on the events leading to and culminating in the death of the thirty-fifth president of the United States of America.

The composition of the commission proves to be more than just interesting. Including Justice Warren, a former Republican office holder but now widely viewed as a progressive, the rest of the commission are an array of what could be construed by most as conservative individuals. They include Richard Russell Jr., a once-mentor of LBJ during his time in the Senate and technically a Democrat, although most southern Democrats of his ilk are Republicans in disguise who run as Democrats only because they would never have been elected as members of the GOP. This is due in no small part to it being considered the party of Lincoln and, hence, no friend of the Deep South. Others are John Sherman Cooper, a Kentucky Republican Senator; Hale Boggs, Democrat, Louisiana Congressman, a man with deep ties to the oil industry; Gerald Ford, Michigan, Republican House Minority Leader; John J. McCloy, head of the CIA; and Allen Welsh Dulles, former head of the CIA.

Arguably, the composition is largely conservative, including the two so-called Democrats. These are not dangerous men who would go out on a limb to threaten the current order, much less want to unearth evidence that cast an even worse light on what had transpired on that fateful November day in Dallas. And to ensure that result, LBJ has included Allen, who will be more adept than his successor, McCloy, at dealing with the loose ends that inevitably will come to the fore. Allen's prominent role in the gathering quickly becomes apparent, having been entrusted to appoint Richard Helms and JJ to oversee the investigatory process.

It comes as some surprise, but out of the blue, Allen asks me to set up a meeting with Helms, excluding JJ. It surprises me that he didn't include JJ and didn't call Richard directly, leaving me to wonder if this is his way of tipping off JJ, his trusted former associate, without telling him in so many words.

I ponder over it for some time without reaching a decision and without mentioning it to JJ.

And then the meeting is upon us.

I know you and Jim don't always see eye-to-eye, particularly of late, Allen tells Helms, who nods in agreement. But it's important that we make sure that he is involved for obvious reasons.

Obvious? Helms asks.

For containment purposes, Dulles tells him. I expect that there is much information that he is privy to about this that neither you nor I know or want to know, and, in that regard, the commission as well.

After some hesitation, Helms agrees.

I suppose so, he allows reluctantly.

With the two of you working together, Dulles continues, he can steer you away if you start heading into dangerous waters, and when he does…

Helms nods.

…you won't need to question why. In fact, you can blame it on him if anything ever comes out to suggest that a full examination was not conducted.

So that's the way it's going to be, Helms says, in resignation.

It's the only way it can be, Dulles reaffirms.

And you'll be there, Allen, to make sure that the commission stays on track.

I will keep them on track, Richard, of that you can be sure.

No one involved in this wants to get started down the wrong path.

No one, he repeats, from Justice Warren to LBJ and Hoover, I can assure you of that.

Even Bobby?

Particularly Bobby. If there's the slightest suggestion that anyone other than Oswald is involved in this, all hell could break loose, and no one, including Bobby, will be able to keep it contained. There will be more than just revelations about Cubans and the Mob conspiring with us. All of the files that have been gathered will be opened, all of the women the president dallied with, the security breaches that occurred; as a result, it will all come under the microscope most intensely in a manner that will sullen America's image for years to come, if not forever.

Helms shakes his head. Women?

Many, many women, Allen reiterates.

Helms pauses, shaking his head in disbelief. I know that it was common knowledge that Kennedy was screwing a few, but....

Not just a few, Richard, for God's sake, Dulles exclaims. He was screwing anybody and everybody he could get his hands on.

Powers was his pimp, bringing him prostitutes from the street, lining up dates, and covering up for female visitors to the White House. There were orgies in Palm Springs, various hotels while he was on the campaign trail, an Admiral's quarters in Hawaii, daily trysts in the White House pool — which, by the way, old Joe paid for — he even had women up into the family quarters. And, apparently, there are photos of the president cavorting with women and other various people, in the nude.

You know that I am not a prude, Richard, but this goes beyond, way beyond simple immorality.

The man could not control himself and didn't appear to even try. He was physically ill with all manner of ailments, including Addison's, syphilis, gonorrhea, or any other such disease, and Dulles pauses and winces. You even could make the argument that he had severe psychological problems.

At this point, Dulles stops to catch his breath.

You know, he was a sitting duck in Dallas, constrained by a brace that held him up straight — the result of one of his late sexual trysts.

Helms appears even more dumbfounded by the vehemence of the arguments being put forward by his former boss, a man known for restraint in pursuing even the most passionate of causes.

No, Dulles begins again; Bobby doesn't want any of this to come out. The death of his brother effectively has cast his image in a manner that suits the family. As things stand now, our former president is considered by many to be a saint.

A saint? Helms exclaims.

Well, no, he's not a saint…of course not, but you know what I mean.

So, we clean up the mess, tidy up any loose ends, and move on, Helms responds after some deliberation.

Yes, we clean up this mess and move on, Dulles concurs. We have no choice. The nation would never forgive us if we did differently. We would be the laughingstock of the world…well, maybe not the laughingstock, but we would be reviled in world opinion if any of this ever gets out.

More than we already are? Helms questions.

Much, much more….

Allen, one last thing.

Yes, Richard, Dulles says wearily.

Have you had this kind of conversation with Jim?

Dulles is in the process of methodically filling his pipe bowl, and the question stops him cold.

I've never discussed it with him, nor will I. Again, he pauses before finally completing the thought. I don't need to, he says with regained assurance.

No, I suppose you don't, Helms concurs.

Our newly appointed chief of Covert Operations in Mexico and Central America, John Moss Whitten, is causing problems for JJ and Richard as they try to shut down what they consider to be a rogue investigation into the death of the president.

Among other things, Whitten, who has been with the company since its inception in 1947, wants a full investigation of JM/WAVE, the covert operations and intelligence-gathering station on the south campus of the University of Miami.

In its short time in operation, it has been the guiding force in "Operation Mongoose," an activity headed by the now departed former air force general, Edward Lansdale, and tasked with overthrowing Fidel Castro. As such, it was involved in the Bay of Pigs disaster as well as providing 'intelligence' during the Cuban Missile Crisis. It has been headed up by George 'Ted' Shackley Jr., one of our most decorated officers and known, due to the color of his hair and mysterious ways, as the "Blond Ghost." He has upwards of 400 agents under his control and, interestingly, a large flotilla of boats, whose purpose, given the location and focus of operations, can only be assumed to involve an invasion, likely an island some 200 nautical miles to the south.

But, more importantly for Whitten is the question of whether JM/WAVE or anyone on its periphery, such as Cuban ex-pats and their ilk, might have been involved with the assassination of JFK.

For obvious reasons, Richard, JJ, and Allen, albeit in the background, one presumes, all want this line of inquiry closed off immediately. Whitten has been heard to decry their maneuvering in moral terms as a "highly reprehensible act." But moral terms, notwithstanding, the act of turning over every stone may not be the key goal of the Warren Commission. Rather, LBJ clearly wants to close off any avenue of discovery and controversy before the first Tuesday of next November, when it is considered by almost everyone as a fait accompli that he will legitimize his presidency with an electoral victory. Whether the report from the commission, due by mid-September, will impact the election remains to be seen, but anyone willing to lay money on that possibility is betting it won't.

1964

The saddest thing about betrayal
is that it never comes from your enemies

The year dawns with a nation still deep in the trauma of losing its highest elected official by assassination. For us, whatever shock we experienced from that tragic day in Dallas has been pushed aside rather quickly by the need to move forward with the investigation into the president's death; for some, that means battening down the hatches.

While bringing JJ up to speed on several developments, I let slip some scuttlebutt I have been hearing about the role of the mob in death.

Maybe it was something Allen inferred prior to Helms arriving for their meeting. Nonetheless, it becomes disturbing when I start asking a few very basic questions.

Carlos Marcello, I begin abruptly, watching JJ for a reaction.

JJ calmly pulls out the perpetually crushed packet of Virginia Slims, lights one, and draws deeply. After exhaling, he looks sadly at me from behind those huge lenses, which pass for glasses.

What have you heard?

That he's a mob chief in New Orleans who had a long-standing beef with the Kennedys.

Long-standing?

Well, ever since the Kennedy administration took office.

So?

I've heard that he once remarked: "The dog will keep biting you if you only cut off its tail. You must cut off the dog's head."

Oh, really?

Apparently, last year, he was telling associates that his need for revenge could be satisfied if only he could find "a nut to take the blame."

A nut? JJ responds.

Yea, a nut...

I hesitate before continuing.

...like Oswald.

This clearly unnerves JJ, who stuffs his cigarette out on his desk, of all places, with unaccustomed gusto.

After some deliberation, he responds.

OK, so what was this guy's beef with Kennedy?

Well, I respond, apparently it was more with Bobby.

Bobby?

Yea, the story making the rounds is that the attorney general had him deported some time ago and dropped in a Guatemalan jungle.

Again, after an extenuated pause, JJ replies with a half-smile forming on his usually impenetrable face.

And this doesn't seem a little far-fetched to you?

I shake my head vigorously, although not sure whether it is in confusion rather than denial.

Who knows what to believe? There are so many ties between Oswald and Marcello.

Like?

At this point, I am beginning to wonder if JJ is really up to speed on the information that I am relaying to him, as opposed to merely stringing me out as he often does in an attempt to learn what I actually know. Nonetheless, I play along.

Apparently, Oswald worked for Marcello in New Orleans from April to October of last year.

Worked directly for Marcello? JJ demands.

No, I respond hesitantly.

But a close associate of his, a David Ferrie and….

And?

Well, I hear that Oswald is apparently a nephew of Dutz Murret, another Marcello associate.

One of their associates….?

Yes. Ferrie or Murret, not sure which one bailed Oswald out of jail after that street disturbance that Oswald got involved in last August. There's also talk about Jack Ruby and that Marcello sent a message to Jimmy Hoffa through an intermediary….

A mob lawyer?

Probably, that Hoffa owes him big time.

JJ jumps on what he thinks is an error or at least an inconsistency.

For arranging to take the president out but not the attorney general who had been causing Hoffa so much grief?

Well, I respond slowly, not quite sure of my footing at this point. With the president gone, it was clear that Bobby...

I pause for a moment.

...won't have the same authority with LBJ, much less remain in the position for long.

JJ starts to laugh.

That, maybe, is the only thing you've got right.

Maurice Oldfield, MI6 Station Chief in Washington, is hosting Arthur Martin, MI5's top counterintelligence interrogator, and Jim Bennett of the RCMP counter-intelligence department. Later in the day, he holds a dinner for the pair and invites JJ, myself, and Ray Rocca, our chief analyst, researcher, and expert on ancient Russian espionage cases, including the Trust and, most recently, Anatoliy Golitsyn.

As is often the case, there is much pre-dinner drinking, mostly whiskey, then lots of wine with our meal, followed by some fine Courvoisier VSOP cognac and an impressive list of liqueurs when we retire to his study.

Maybe it's because of the amount of drink consumed and the fact that alcoholism contributed to his death at an early age, but the talk turns to the late Wisconsin Senator Joseph McCarthy and his obsession with communism, which he claimed was rampant in the American institutions in the fifties.

McCarthy ascended to national status following an otherwise unnoteworthy stint as a circuit judge and brief service in the latter stages of World War Two, when he engineered a stunning primary victory over the then-notable incumbent, Sen. Robert M. LaFollettee Jr, who had held office since 1925. His victory — largely a result of claiming falsely that La Follette had profited by not serving in the war even though the senator was 46 at the time of Pearl Harbor —

served as a warning of what would follow once he became a senator.

In addition to his years of Senate service, Lafollette Jr. was the son of "Fighting Bob" LaFollette, who represented Wisconsin in the Senate and the House of Representatives and was elected the 20th governor of Wisconsin.

Clearly, defeating a member of the LaFollette family by misrepresentation and innuendo heralded the introduction of one of our most troubling periods. McCarthy's unsubstantiated claims of communist infiltration into the heart of American government and service cast a dark shadow over the nation for a considerable period of time, despite being denounced by most mainstream politicians as well as President Dwight D. Eisenhower.

Nonetheless, now, seven years after his death, there remains a hard-core base of supporters, including, to my astonishment, JJ as well as Rocca. During the conversation, both fervently defended McCarthy, believing his efforts helped to increase security in the U.S.

Things take a turn for the worse when Bennett makes the mistake of expressing sympathy for the many victims of McCarthy's extremism. Rocca, who has consumed way too much alcohol, takes a swing at him. Fortunately, the many years he has spent behind a desk reviewing past history makes him incapable of delivering a punch at the best of times.

The discussion that ensues prompts Bennett to observe that neither JJ nor Rocca appear capable of differentiating between European-style socialists and hard-core communists.

Eventually, tempers cool, but it is a learning experience for me, as I never viewed McCarthy as a legitimate political entity.

Nonetheless, I consider it prudent not to voice my opinions on the matter, at least not in the company of JJ or Rocca.

Again, JJ is missing for an unusual amount of time. Word has it that another Soviet defector, Yuriy Ivanovich Nosenko, has fallen into our lap…or has he? That is a critically unresolved issue from day one.

He arrived like his former colleague, Anatoliy Golitsyn, in the heart of winter, but unlike Anatoliy, Nosenko has received nothing close to the hero's welcome that greeted Golitsyn. Initially, he is held in a safe house but subsequently has been moved to a specially constructed jail in a remotely wooded area, likely in Maryland or Virginia. Very few of us know for sure where he is, and those who do, such as JJ, aren't talking.

What is known is that he was extremely nervous in his first meeting with JJ, asking for upwards of four shots of whiskey in short order to calm himself down, not unlike his compatriot, Nosenko, something that should have allowed him to bond with JJ. But clearly, that is not the case.

Nosenko initially offered his services to us in Geneva in 1962, claiming to be the deputy chief of the Seventh Department of the KGB. But instead of immediately spiriting him to the west, he was told he would be paid a retainer of $25,000 per year and asked to carry on in place.

Not sure how well that might have worked out, but by the start of this year he was expressing concerns that he had been uncovered and needed to defect immediately.

Aside from his worries about being burned, Nosenko claimed to have pertinent information about the death of our president, including the revelation that the KGB had conducted surveillance of Oswald but had never tried to recruit him because he was considered mentally unstable. As much as this claim might be reassuring, there is some thought that the Russians could be using Nosenko to try and cover up any potential involvement, fearing that if it were found that they were complicit in the killing, it would start a nuclear war.

To complicate matters further, Nosenko subsequently admits that he had not been found out by the KGB and had lied in an effort to persuade us to accelerate his defection.

All of this only further clouds the issues surrounding Golitsyn's defection and the Kennedy assassination for many people in our ranks, but not JJ.

Long after I have fallen asleep, the phone rings, and I stumble with it. There is heavy breathing for what seems like an eternity, but, in reality, it is probably little more than a half-minute. Finally, the breathing turns to words.

Are you awake now? I hear JJ intone cautiously.

Yes, I reply wearily.

He begins to ruminate about the commission.

I interrupt him.

Are you sure we should be talking about this over the phone?

It's alright, he assures me. I have both of our phones swept regularly.

As recently as today in my case.

And mine? I query.

Probably about a week ago, he responds.

A lot could have happened in the interim, I reply. You don't know who is tapping phones these days...I mean the FBI, LBJ...even the Soviets.

I've been having your phone and various residences swept for countless years now, and nothing has ever turned up....

For how long? I demand.

Don't be offended. It was for your protection as well as mine. By the way, I've never tapped it during that time.

Tapped it? I sputtered in amazement. My God.

Don't act so disgusted. You've known all this time that I have the authority to tap any phone.

Anyone in the firm, I correct him.

I suppose so if you want to split hairs, he says with a rare, wry chuckle.

That's the directive that Dulles gave you as director. By the way, has it been renewed?

There is a silence at the other end.

Has it been renewed? I repeat.

It's never been rescinded.

I wonder how that got by McCone?

I don't believe it was a written directive, JJ allows after a long pause. Besides, Allen never objected to me gathering info about those outside of the company, either.

Yes, he rather liked the dirt you were able to dig up on some of the capital's notables, among others, during your fishing expeditions, even though it was clearly illegal.

JJ chuckles. Nor did it offend his Presbyterian sensibilities, he allows.

On that light note, he disengages, leaving me to wonder about the real purpose of his call and my superior's increasingly erratic behavior.

It's becoming a bit of a disturbing pattern, not the least of which is how it impacts my ability to get a good night's sleep, but JJ calls me yet again late at night. Rather than turn on the light and struggle with the phone while my eyes adjust, I snatch it off the receiver and sink back into the bed, listening in the darkness.

This discussion appears to be even less salient than some of our more recent ones.

Initially, he begins by quoting from a Frost poem about two roads diverging.

I took the one less traveled by...

...and that has made all the difference.

Before I can ask him about the significance of this couplet, he begins to ramble on about the early days, in particular Kim Philby, Guy Burgess, Donald Maclean and others.

You know, he tells me, at one juncture in this wandering recollection of his past relationships, when speaking with Philby, I never called him by his nickname. He was always Adrian to me.

How did he become known as Kim? I ask.

There is a long pause, accompanied by sporadic bursts of heavy breathing. At this point, I'm not sure whether he is fixing himself more drinks, lighting yet another cigarette or has simply fallen asleep.

And then, in a monotone, he resumes our discourse, leading me to believe that he had been consulting his file cards.

Harold Adrian Russell Philby was born in the Punjab, the son of a British diplomat, JJ relates. He was given his nickname by his father, based on the protagonist in the Rudyard Kipling novel, *Kim*....

More silence.

...you know, he resumes, he might as well have been a fictional character. When you become familiar with his life story, it's amazing how many occasions he dodged the proverbial bullet.

Really? I respond, deciding to humor him.

Oh, yes. Our Kim has lived a charmed existence.

More lives than a cat, I would say.

I remain silent and so JJ plows on.

During the Spanish Civil War, he was masquerading as a fascist sympathizer in the guise of a war correspondent.... JJ laughs at the apparent absurdity of the notion. In fact, his reports were so favorable that Francisco Franco personally awarded him the Red Cross of Military Merit.

Red, I interject, that's rather apropos.

I suppose so, JJ chuckles yet again.

He was in a car with several other correspondents in 1937 when a shell exploded just in front of it. Three of his colleagues were killed, two of them American, a fellow from the AP, one from Newsweek and another wire service reporter. I believe it was Reuters.

There's a pause as JJ re-collects himself.

Somehow, Philby escaped with little more than a scratch.

My silence encourages him to continue.

By the way, he was already employed by the Soviets and was, I have since heard, sending his covert reports in the form of love letters to a fictional Paris belle. He pauses for what seems like an interminable amount of time.

And, I finally interject.

Well, it turns out the address for the letters provided by his Soviet masters was 78 Rue de Grenelle.

Another pause.

And what is its significance? I ask somewhat brusquely.

JJ laughs again. More heartily this time.

It's the address of the Soviet embassy. Anyone really checking him out could have easily discovered that.

So, he was lucky, and, I add, quite possibly, the Russians are not really as clever as we usually give them credit for.

That assertion stumps JJ momentarily but, nonetheless, is discarded.

At one point, the Soviets apparently wanted Philby to assassinate the generalissimo, but in typical fashion, it appears that he must have refused. He told me once, well before I even began to suspect him of betrayal, that he was somewhat of a coward.

I suppose, I interject, that such a declaration was intended to throw you off his scent. After all, a coward would never volunteer for something as hazardous as being a spy, would he?

I'm not quite sure of that, JJ says after some contemplation.

Being a spy is, in some sense, the work of a coward.

Not wishing to argue with him, given the hour, I press JJ for other examples of Philby's many lives.

Well, aside from escaping death, the most noteworthy involves the situation just after the war when an officer of what we now call the KGB decided to defect and hinted that he would be able to provide the names of Soviet agents in the upper ranks of the British Secret Service, which presumably included Philby or if just Donald Maclean and Guy Burgess, nonetheless it would point the finger at Kim.

Quite probably, I reply.

Philby was assigned to bring him in.

Oh, no! I exclaim.

Yea, JJ says with a sigh. Of all the people they could pick. And it wasn't just the good fortune of drawing the assignment. Lady luck also intervened in the form of Mother Nature as the plane carrying Philby to Istanbul to take custody of the defector was delayed by bad weather. That gave the Russkies, presumably having been given the heads up by Philby, enough time to scoop the defector up and whisk him back to Moscow. By the way, the British ambassador was asleep at the switch at the time.

How's that? I ask.

He was off on his yacht in the Bosporus, just lazing away as only the Brits can do. So, attempts to have him take in the defector went for naught.

Hmm, that's two pieces of good fortune, I interject.

Well, there's more. Kim was fortunate to be in Washington, working with me, among others, when we started to piece together information about what turned out to be a ring of agents in high places in MI5, Six, and other British agencies.

My silence continues to spur him on.

He was able to warn both Maclean and Burgess, who was living with him at the time and carrying on in a most discreditable fashion, I might add, given the sexual orientation of the pair of them. Their ability to make a hasty escape eventually cast suspicion on Philby, but the very fact that they were not subject to a rigorous interrogation delayed the unmasking of my good friend Kim for a considerable time.

Yea, and Philby managed to stave off his British minders for the better part of a couple of years, I add, most of which time he was under house arrest or something like that.

There is an explosion of wind at the other end of the line as if the very life is being sucked out of JJ's lungs.

I would have liked to have a crack at him, JJ finally allows, and I was not alone in that regard.

I know for sure that Bill, ah, Harvey, would have liked a shot at him, too. Absolutely!

So, Philby dodged yet another bullet?

Well, as I said, he has lived a charmed existence, JJ allows.

And you never had any earlier suspicions?

Again, silence prevails for what seems like the longest time.

Finally, there is a long sigh.

In retrospect, I should have put two and two together as early as 1946.

How's that? I ask.

I knew Philby back then from our time together during the war. We were, by that time, the best of buddies.

Right.

Philby, like many in the British service, was awarded some honor, OBE, I believe.

Order of the British Empire, I interject.

Yea, something like that. Anyway, we are out celebrating it and good old Kim is knocking back the whiskey in fine form when he lets slip that Britain could do with a "stiff dose of proper socialism."

And by proper you thought he might mean communism?

Well, it did cross my mind a day or two later when I was able to better recollect the events of the night in question.

Oh, you were hung over then, were you?

Hung over? Never! I prefer to think that I was merely somewhat indisposed.

Have it your way, I concede, then changing the subject, I ask him about something that has been gnawing away at me for some time.

Why do you think that it was all of these upper-class Brits who betrayed their country and us in the process?

He doesn't respond immediately, so I carry on.

Most of our traitors come from a lesser social order. Working-class folk or lower middle class. They believe in communism because it is consistent with their hopes based on their life experiences. In many respects, they or their family members suffered grievous wrongs under capitalism.

Privilege can be a millstone as well as a boon, JJ finally responds. Besides, when you have everything handed to you, just like our late president, it's easy to become contemptuous, to believe that you can do whatever you want without regard for the consequences.

And you believe that of JFK.

I don't just believe that. I know it to be true. And, by the way, so do you.

So, did that cause you to evaluate him and his presidency in a different light?

It would be hard not to. And, as you well know, I am not alone in that regard.

Maybe it was the hour or all of the time that I had dwelled on it of late, the nagging suspicions, but before I could even contemplate what I was saying, the unspeakable jumped out of my mouth.

And you weren't about to make the same mistake with him as you did with Philby?

Silence ensues. Not even a hint of heavy breathing. And then, the beeping sound that is consistent with the action of a receiver at one end of the line hanging up.

You've got to watch what you're saying over the phone, JJ tells me the next day.

You've already assured me that they are safe. Told me that on several occasions, I respond.

Well, you never know; one can't be too cautious, he says.

Although I think I should leave, JJ seems to be in no hurry to dispense with my services.

Unopened files clutter his desk, but he makes no move to work with them, which is usually a sign for me to take my leave.

Finally, he speaks.

For years, we have been searching for the missing link, the fourth man in London — possibly Anthony Blunt — but, more importantly, has there been a mole here in Washington.... Does he, she, even exist?

Or, is it just a clever counterintuitive ploy on the Soviets' part to deceive and confuse us, in particular, me? That, more than anything, is the issue that continues to haunt me....

Is Goltisyn the ultimate in disinformation? I suddenly interject.

No, no, that can't be, he says in a horrified tone. Golitsyn gives me structure....

And what about Philby...?

Philby tortures me.

You trusted him.

Implicitly. At least initially.

And...?

JJ sinks deeper into his chair, smoke from an ever-present Virginia Slim building around his head in a futile attempt to camouflage the torture he is enduring.

He drains his coffee cup of bourbon and stares at the wall in front of him, now oblivious to my presence...imprisoned in his personal hell.

Maybe, he allows at long last, maybe I am the fifth man.

I am aghast at such an absurd notion and scarcely able to believe my ears.

How…how can that be? I manage to stutter.

Not by inclination, he reassures me, but by design. A Trojan Horse without knowing it.

The Soviets turned me by using the tools of the trade that I had mastered to work against me, knowing that the unmasking of Philby would drive me further than reason or logic dictated.

You can't blame yourself for being suspicious under the circumstances.

And if the Soviets were…are playing me....

The notion is left dangling.

I think you give them too much credit, I try to assure him. They have their own concerns.

Huh?

They have no principles; they have betrayed everything that the Russian Revolution stood for, in the process destroying many committed party members...surely even the most dedicated communists can see that.

I pause to allow a rebuttal, but when none is forthcoming, I continue. Whereas we are still living the dream that the American Revolution made possible. We are not perfect, but our ideals are, although I suppose, the Russians might say the same about theirs, but can they justify their current practices, vis-a-vis ours?

But JJ is not about to be dissuaded by me, and he returns to his newly found conviction, probably aided by Golitsyn, that the KGB has succeeded over time in planting numerous double agents amongst those recruited by us and the FBI in 1958 and 1959.

What do your FBI sources tell you? I ask.

They are as much confused as I am, he responds after a lengthy silence. But of a greater concern, it appears that I won't be hearing anything of value from them in the future, he adds.

What?

In effect, Hoover has declared me persona non grata.

Really?

He doesn't like being told that he has been fooled. He's simply not prepared to accept that, so he's told those in contact with us that they should no longer cooperate with me.

And, they'll do that, even your good friend, Sam Papich?

Oh, most certainly. Hoover is a tremendously vindictive man. Agents are terrified of incurring his displeasure, no matter how trivial the offense, perceived or otherwise. So, yes, the pool is drying up rapidly. In fact, I suspect it has bottomed out.

This is bad!

Oh, it's worse than bad, and it doesn't stop there. The conflict between me and the Directorate of Operations over the success, or lack of it, of their intelligence-gathering efforts, which I have been increasingly questioning, has come to a head. They are accusing me of causing a paralysis of a sort by virtue of simply casting aspersions about some of their assets.

Well, surely, you can convince them. Lay out your concerns, your rationale, provide evidence.

Oh, no, no, no, he responds alarmingly. It's never that simple. I can't, nor should I, divulge all of my cards. It's like poker, only the stakes are so much higher. So very much higher.

Later, I am forced to consider the possibility that the stakes JJ referred to may have little to do with the security of the nation but rather JJ's status with the higher-ups, a situation that had been deteriorating ever since he lost the protection of his patron, Allen Dulles.

There are more challenging times for Frank Gardiner Wisner. Since being recalled from London, Wisner's health and mental state have spiraled even farther downward, if that is possible.

There are hints that he has attempted suicide or contemplated it.

When I broach the subject with JJ, he looks even more distressed than usual.

He pauses to light a cigarette and starts to speak, only to be interrupted by a hacking cough which appears to be more persistent these days.

Hunched over his desk, JJ again appears to be withdrawing within himself.

Poor Frank, he finally allows. Never got over Hungary.

Why is that? I ask.

Frank headed up the directorate responsible for Hungary at the time. Richard was his chief of operations.

Helms?

JJ shakes his head in the affirmative.

We had been using Radio Free Europe actively to encourage rebellions and other disruptive actions within the satellite states such as Poland, Czechoslovakia, East Germany, and Hungary. The latter was definitely the most likely candidate for something to happen.

Again, I ask, why?

Something to do with the makeup of the Magdyrs. Who knows?

Regardless of the student movement, you have to remember that all this occurred after Khrushchev had denounced Stalin in a secret gathering of the Twentieth Party Congress six or seven months earlier....

Which you helped make public.

I had a role, no doubt. Anyway, under Stalinist policies, Hungary had become one of the more repressive states — probably because the Magdyrs were extremely difficult to control.

Faint traces of a grim smile form at the corners of his thin lips

The student movement was growing, and I guess it all just came together on that October afternoon when about 20,000 protesters, most of them students and writers, mobilized at the Bem Statute.

Bem?

General Bem…ironically a Polish general but the hero of Hungary's War of Independence some one hundred years earlier. Well, you know how these things work. There are speeches, I think they sang the national anthem, which was banned at the time; then someone hoisted the new Hungarian flag with the hammer and sickle cut out of the middle.

This must have been very inflammatory, particularly in a Soviet state, I venture.

Indeed, JJ acknowledges, then continues.

One thing led to another, and by late afternoon, the mob — I shouldn't use that word — the liberationists…

Is that a real word? I wonder aloud, but JJ just ignores me

…had moved on to their parliament building and had swelled in numbers to over 200,000 people. Quite remarkable, really, and up to that point, they are very peaceful although increasingly…spirited.

Things take a turn for the worse? I ask.

No, no, no, you silly person, they take a turn for the better, JJ corrects me.

Some high official in the government, the first secretary or whatever, broadcasts a speech condemning the demands, but it only serves to inflame the crowd further. At this point, a small group decides to demonstrate their patriotism, and they take to toppling the statue of Stalin that had been erected there a few years earlier. A church was demolished to make way for it, I believe.

Where's the military, their secret police? I ask.

That's an interesting point. The AVH, Hungary's answer to the KGB, certainly was as hated, if not more. Hundreds of thousands of people disappeared during the height of the Stalinist atrocities that dominated Hungary since we deserted them and all the other Soviet satellite nations in the aftermath of the Second World War.

That's a strong statement, I respond.

But true, JJ replies. In fact, you might say it's even a little understated.

Silence envelopes the room as JJ catches his breath, before continuing.

As it turns out, the AVH was tied up with a separate demonstration at the Radio Budapest building, where a substantial group had gathered in the hopes of broadcasting their demands. As I recall, the AVH opened fire on the demonstrators and then called in the Hungarian military to support them. But instead, the army sided with the demonstrators. Some of them even tore off the red stars from their caps as a sign of support for the protestors.

And the Soviets? I ask.

Tanks were called in, but by then, the resistance had seized the moment, using Molotov cocktails, in particular, to negate the effectiveness of the tanks. There were ongoing skirmishes within Budapest itself for days on end, but then some commanders started negotiating local cease-fires. It was all quite remarkable. By the end of the month, fighting had ceased, the Soviets had withdrawn to the countryside, even the border, and negotiations were taking place between Hungarian leaders and the Russians.

And where were we?

On the sidelines, watching. Frank was beside himself. He desperately wanted us to move troops in or at least make a public announcement that we would join the fray if the Soviets tried to escalate hostilities.

But we didn't. It was all rather sad. Also, this is all happening just days before our own election. So, I suppose Ike felt hamstrung to do anything even though it was very clear that he was going to win in a landslide for the second time against Stevenson. Also, the thinking making the rounds was that we were in no position to support any military action, and the last thing any elected official wanted to be seen doing was precipitating a nuclear war.

So, we sat on our hands?

That's about it, JJ says with a sigh. Somehow, the Russians got a transcript or just the gist of the discussion held by Eisenhower in which he told the military in no uncertain terms that there would be no real support for the uprising other than moral support.

How did the Russians find out about that?

Clearly, they had a mole in place, someone with access.

My jaw drops noticeably.

It's the only explanation!

The only explanation? I respond. Not a reporter, digging around....

JJ ignores my question and continues with his narrative.

Well, the Soviets were negotiating with the Hungarian leaders, who were, by the way, card-carrying communists.

There was every reason to believe that the Russkies were prepared to withdraw and let Hungary set up its own regime. And then, suddenly, troops and tanks were back, moving on Budapest. Some of the Hungarian leaders involved in the negotiations were being detained and, well…we now know how it all turned out.

But they didn't need a mole to tell them that the U.S. was not going to get involved, I note. They could probably have read about it in the papers.

You can believe what you want, but I'm telling you how I see it.

We sit in silence for several minutes, JJ puffing furiously on yet another cigarette.

Finally, I break the silence.

I suppose it's not really unlike how we've handled the Cuba situation. In fact, you could say it was even worse since the Hungarians had their own army on their side.…

JJ looks at me with disgust although it's not entirely clear who or what it is directed at, but I continue, nonetheless.

You know we are isolationists at heart. Didn't want to get involved from the get-go in either of the First or Second World Wars.

That all changed, JJ lectures, with a wagging finger.

After the Second World War, we've had no choice. Faced with the communist threat, we are the only ones capable of taking them on. But we're always doing it with one hand tied behind our backs.

Huh? I snort.

Because we're a democracy, damn it. We're fighting a totalitarian regime that silences its internal opponents, often in the most brutal fashion. And, yet, those of us waging the good fight have to answer to individuals who either don't understand the magnitude of the situation or are too interested in their own political careers to see the big picture.

I am stunned and yet not surprised by the vehemence of JJ's remarks, and he continues.

That's why some of us think we have to do more than we have done in the past if we want this country to survive....

I can only blink my eyes in amazement.

Think about it, JJ posits. Half of the world's population — it might even be more with the way China continues to grow — is under totalitarian control, aligned against everything we stand for as a nation. And who do we have in support?

With no response from myself, JJ continues.

Great Britain? A country beset by labor strife and in such sorry financial condition that it is restricting the amount of currency its citizens can take out of the country.

Yes, the Beatles would agree with you.

The what?

They're a new British rock group that, among others, are upset with those currency restrictions.

Rock group? This causes JJ to look blankly at me for a spell before returning to the thread that I had interrupted.

Then there's France. If you listen to her politicians, you'd think we're the enemy rather than the country that rode to her rescue, liberating her from the yoke of fascism.

Twice, we've helped free the French, but that cuts no slack with them.

I have to nod my head in agreement.

All we've got is the Canadians and the Australians, and, as you well know, the Canadians want to be peacekeepers, not defenders. In fact, they have some leaders who might as well be communists if they aren't already card-carrying members.

That's a little harsh, don't you think? After all, the Canadians acquitted themselves quite nicely in both wars if I understand my history properly.

Oh, I'm not talking about the average Johnny Canuck. They're as good as anybody. It's their leadership, I question; that and the country's French factor.

What?

Very few of them voluntarily participated in the last big war, and most of them had to be dragged into it...some sort of conscription row...I don't know all of the details, except that it was a troublesome situation that never really worked itself out.

Right, I believe their prime minister at the time...

Some guy named King, JJ volunteers with a sneer.

Yes, William Lyon Mackenzie King. He issued one of the most astounding political statements at the time. Something to the effect: "Conscription, if necessary; not necessarily conscription."

JJ begins to laugh at the absurdity of the statement before continuing.

The bottom line is that Canada can't be counted on right now. Why, even in our last go-round over Cuba, the Canadian government was one of the few holdouts in giving us unqualified support.

Diefenbaker, I volunteer.

Who?

The Canadian prime minister at the time, I explain.

Oh, yes.

He has something in common with you.

What's that?

He doesn't trust Kennedy, either.

Oh, right, right. I recall that there was a bit of a contretemps during a visit by the late president to Ottawa.

Yes, I continue, there was a lack of commitment from Mr. Diefenbaker over putting nuclear weapons on Canadian soil as part of their NORAD commitment.

Hmmm...it sounds familiar.

At some point, Kennedy scrawled a derogatory comment on a document that wound up in the prime minister's hands.

Oh?

Something to the effect of 'Now what do I do with the old bastard?'

JJ laughs so hard, a rarity these days, that he begins to choke.

And the president couldn't pronounce his name properly.

What, Diefenbocker?

You see, that's wrong. It's baker, Diefenbaker, not bocker.

Bocker, baker...why are you so interested in this?

Oh, somewhere in my lineage, there's a Canadian connection.

Hmmm. That explains a lot of things.

What! I exclaim.

But JJ is already back deep into his files.

A waiting car at the recently renamed Tucson International Airport whisks me 59 miles down US Route 89, following the Santa Cruz River, to just north of the border town of Nogales, where JJ has holed up on a ranch that belongs to a member of his mother's side of the family. His wife, Cicely, prefers the more comfortable Tucson and has returned to an estate there owned by her father.

The Southwest is a remarkable area, JJ tells me as we watch the sun setting on the stony inclines, changing them to a magnificent purple-pink hue. I am shivering as the temperature has easily dropped some ten to fifteen degrees in less than an hour from its mid-winter day high of 72. It will get even colder as we progress through the night, reaching as low as freezing in the early morning hours before beginning its ascent back into the seventies once the sun rises again.

JJ has a drink in one hand and a Virginia Slim in the other, ironically oblivious to the contradiction that is smoking in the fresh outdoors.

This land, he observes, waving his arm and cigarette in a sweeping motion from the border area northward to the tracts of desert and mountains that comprise southern Arizona, is, he pauses to contemplate his description…magnificently desolate.

I have to concur. From what I have seen in my limited travel from Tucson, the vistas stretch for miles of unimpeded broken rock and dirt interspersed with cactus and brush. For an easterner accustomed to cultivated, verdant, parkland settings resplendent with magnificent strands of trees, the Southwest takes a little getting used to. Nonetheless, it takes one's breath away.

I think it's understandable, that aside from the family connection to the area, there is something about it that draws JJ back, much like his love of fly fishing. Here, he explores caves and the nooks and crannies of the area, searching for gemstones that he polishes to perfection and fashions into cuff links or other gifts for his friends. They are akin to the nuggets of counterintelligence that cross his desk back at the office, shining brightly once he is finished with them.

During dinner, including copious drinks, JJ's spirits seemed to decline in direct proportion to the diminished light and the increased consumption of alcohol. Aside from complementing the staff made up of local men of Hispanic origin, not unlike his mother, for much of the meal he has been morose and withdrawn.

During these quiet moments, I recall one of my rare conversations with his wife, Cicely d'Autremont, with whom he has a son, James Charles Angleton, and two daughters, Truffy and Lucy d'Autremont.

Jim, she recalled, is very much like his grandmother Mercedes, affectionately known as Mamache — a very intuitive and emotional woman. Both, Cicely insisted, are fatalists. But that aside, she also likened him to being both a Latino and an Apache, hence, a gut fighter.

Somehow, I find that difficult to comprehend, given the deterioration of his health and appearance.

Nonetheless, now, with a Kir in his hand — a French concoction consisting of crème de cassis, a black-currant liqueur, topped up with white wine — which he seems to enjoy both before and after dinners, he is reflective in a manner rarely experienced.

Our conversation ranges on all matters of things from the troubles he is experiencing with Yuriy Ivanovich Nosenko, who, increasingly, he is convinced is a double agent, to his difficulties in reconciling the policies of our late president, notwithstanding his death.

But what if you, ah, we, are wrong? I finally venture.

Surprisingly, JJ chuckles.

What if, as you didn't say, I, we, are right?

What's worse?

Being wrong and acting on it or being right and doing nothing?

I don't know? I answer, shaking my head.

I do, JJ responds with more certainty than I have seen in some time.

But why, I wonder, is JJ in Arizona that night, much less for what reason did he bring me here?

Had he been to Mexico City? Checking out some of the theories that have been making the rounds while the official investigation into the death of the president winds down.

Or is he simply worn out and in need of a sunny respite in the land of his ancestors?

At some point, one has to wonder: Who is fooling whom? Has it come to the point where JJ is no longer capable of discerning what is real and what is disinformation? Or, is it even more than that, despite his earlier suggestion that he may have involuntarily been duped by the Russians? Is that part of a cover-up to throw me off his scent? Is he, dare I even think it, a double agent...one of the Soviet moles who he, ostensibly, has based his entire career attempting to root out? These are the dark questions that increasingly keep me awake at night.

From what I can observe, the combination of alcohol, social and professional isolation, insomnia, stress, and obsessive suspicion is making JJ increasingly unstable. Paranoia is evident. For him, it appears that it is better to have a clear, organized, conspiratorial view of the world than to have the chaos that doubt and conflicting evidence inevitably seeds.

Isolated in his secure, dark offices on the second floor, the dangers of delusional cross-breeding and infection are severe.

From what I have begun to learn and understand, paranoia is an adoptive mechanism. It develops a defense against insignificance and being ignored. A paranoid's mindset is that he/she is maintaining a lonely vigil and pursuing a lonely task, searching for confirmatory evidence.

There is much talk that Golitsyn and JJ share the same malady. Like JJ, Golitsyn has a messianic quality to him and can weave disparate pieces of information and happenings together into a seemingly coherent subplot, which otherwise has escaped everyone else. To both of them, there is no such thing as coincidence.

Many times, JJ has stipulated that one of the keys to success in this complex craft, beyond knowing what the enemy is up to, is finding out how our tactics are working on them. He calls it 'playback.' But the question that nags me is: How do we know if playback is working if JJ and the Russia section are not working together? It's a question that I doubt I will ever be able to answer satisfactorily.

My concerns are amplified during a chance encounter with one of our top officials who tells me about a lengthy discussion he had with JJ over drinks recently.

Listening to him, the official notes, was not unlike what you might experience examining an impressionist painting. To an uninformed viewer, the work seems incoherent.

I press him to expand, and he tells me that he has come to the conclusion that JJ has a devious quality, which is amplified by his allusiveness — a description that causes me to laugh out loud.

He looks sharply at me.

Well, I explain, in part it's the nature of the work but, I concede, also the man.

I understand, he allows after some contemplation, but the reasoning for so many of his conclusions seem, to put it bluntly, quite flimsy — lacking in any substance. Jim can carry on forever, always suggesting that there is a great deal that he is privy to but, unfortunately, not able to tell you.

And it leaves you wondering whether his work is little more than smoke and mirrors and like the *Wizard of Oz*, in that there is nothing behind the curtain of secrecy that surrounds him and his department.

After several moments of silence, he adds, I am not the only one who is beginning to have doubts about our head of counterintelligence and the work he claims to have done over the years.

To the average person, the circumstances surrounding the death of Mary Pinchot Meyer are difficult to comprehend. Here, you have an obscure artist, albeit a person of some social connections, out for a noon-day walk along the waterway near her studio — only to be shot in the head, assassination-style, for no apparent reason.

Of course, those of us in the know — aware that, at the time of the president's death, Mary was his favored mistress — are immediately on guard.

Is there info she was privy to about the late president that people don't want to come out? What about her former husband, Cord? There's no question that he was unhappy with her relationship with the president despite their divorce. Could he have been responsible in some way? Then, there's the question of what she knew about Cord's work in the Company.

Still, it's almost a year since the death of the president. Why would anyone, or any organization for that matter, wait that long to quiet a potentially dangerous witness?

Police immediately arrest a Negro named Crump, who was fishing nearby at the time and who makes matters worse for himself by providing conflicting versions of what he was doing when Mary was killed. Still, there is no weapon, no robbery, no apparent motive for him to have killed her. As always, the way police treat colored folk, in general, might explain his difficulties in explaining his whereabouts at the time.

Clearly, the murder has all the earmarks of a professional job. But...by whom? Certainly not Mr. Crump.

That night, before I fall asleep, I hear Mary's last tape playing over and over again in my head as I lie there in the darkness. She is talking to a friend, and the fear in her voice is palpable. She says that she knows that people have been in her townhouse/studio: Windows open that she remembered closing, an item of clothing out of place in one of her drawers, but more than just the physical evidence, she senses that things are closing in around her.

Why would people be in your studio? The caller asks.

I know too much, Mary replies.

About what? The caller asks.

Our late president: What he was thinking about for America and the world when that terrible thing happened to him.

There is silence as the caller obviously struggles with the implications of Mary's statement.

Do you mean different than what we are hearing — the stories about the investigation?

Maybe, she says, after some consideration.

Have you been called before the commission and testified?

No, Mary tells her, they don't want to hear from me.

Do they know about you?

Oh, yes, Mary responds quietly, they know everything about me.

And now she is dead, execution-style, while out on a what appears to be an innocent mid-day stroll.

I am left to wonder: Was the intruder JJ, someone else, or has there been more than one intruder? My curiosity is further piqued upon discovering that our wiretap had been shut down within hours of the shooting. Later, I learn that Ben Bradlee and his wife, Tony, Mary's sister, found JJ in the Georgetown townhouse after the shooting, apparently looking for her diary.

Also, more significantly, is Mary dead because of what was overheard in that last tape, or earlier ones?

People are after the diary, JJ tells me in an offhand way, almost immediately after her death.

Us?

I am greeted with a blank, vacant stare

People associated with the Kennedys? The FBI?

He grimaces. You know I can't say much.

Nonetheless, others are not as reluctant to talk about it, with many expressing an interest in Mary's diary in the wake of her...assassination? Calling it simply a murder does not seem appropriate. Regardless, her sister, Tony, and husband, Ben Bradlee, have visited her townhouse/studio on several occasions, discovering JJ on at least one of those trips. How many times he has been there, both now and before her death, is a question that goes unanswered.

At one point, we are sitting in JJ's inner sanctum. He is holding a variety of photos of Mary and various people who have intersected her life. One appears to include her and another woman. I can only see it from across JJ's desk, but they are riding in a golf cart while a resolute JFK, albeit smiling for the camera, marches ahead of them in pursuit of his next shot, or should we say conquest?

Then there is the photo he passes me of a young Mary and Cord, in uniform but before he suffered his disfiguring facial injury. She is staring at him intently, clearly in love.

Obviously, you've never seen Cord before his injury, JJ allows, taking note of my apparently intense examination of the photo.

He is tall and extremely fit, with what appears to be slightly wavy hair.

I thought Mary and Cord hooked up after Cord was injured in the war.

Oh, no, JJ says dismissively before resuming his narrative.

They both had pacifist views when they married in '45. At least, that's what Cord led Mary to believe. Both attended the UN Conference...the one in San Fran that led to the founding of the United Nations.

I suspect that what I am about to hear is not much different from what JJ had told me earlier when the subject of Mary's liaison with the president and their use of LSD was raised. Has he forgotten that extended briefing, or is he simply trying to deal with the pain of her death and the possibility that he may have, overtly or otherwise, some responsibility? Nonetheless, I am obliged to listen yet again.

Cord was an aide of Harold Stassen, the former governor of Minnesota and, over time, a perpetually unsuccessful Republican candidate for presidency. Mary was supposedly covering the conference as a reporter for a newspaper syndication service. I can't or don't know which one. He shakes his head vigorously. It doesn't matter.

I lean forward to signal my interest in hearing more, still clutching the photo firmly, in the hopes that he might reveal new info.

Well, JJ pauses to take a swig from the coffee cup, which I am now totally convinced has little familiarity with coffee.

Cord became president of the United World Federalists in 1947. In that role, Cord regularly visited colleges and universities, encouraging support...

JJ catches himself with a smile.

...and, enjoying, I am given to understand the benefits, if you can call it that, of being a disfigured war hero.

Ah, yes, I acknowledge. Those benefits that you have mentioned before.

JJ nods appreciatively, seemingly unaware that we have

been down this path before.

Well, apparently many a young, sweet thing took pity on this war hero who now saw the error of his ways.

Yes, they took pity, as you have said.

JJ looks at me suspiciously. You know what I mean. There were many willing to assuage his pain, ah, physically.

Yes, not unlike our late president, who was always seeking comfort from his pain.

Well, not quite like him, c'mon now, JJ responds sharply.

He pauses again to ease his parched throat as well as light yet another cigarette.

At some point, JJ continues, he came to our attention. Allen claims it wasn't until '51 but it wouldn't surprise me if it was much earlier, he adds.

Why?

The narrative was that Cord had seen the error of his ways.

Oh, so it wouldn't look as good if he had always been an anti-peacenik.

Well, JJ allows, it would have certainly helped him when he came into the crosshairs of Senator McCarthy.

Yes, I concur. It didn't look good for him for a while, what with the Wisconsin senator painting him with his wide-reaching Communist brush.

JJ scowls at the apparent disparagement of McCarthy.

OK, I concede, so Allen and Helms came to his rescue, vouching for him at some point.

Maybe it's the expression on my face or reminders that we have been down this path before that snaps JJ back into the present.

Clearly, our side trip into personal matters has stretched the limits of JJ's tolerance, and he waves for me to return the photo.

Then rises to signal my departure.

Still, I am mindful of some of the gossip that I had heard previously about JJ and his apparent infatuation with Mary.

So, it comes as little surprise when I learn that it is JJ who had gained possession of this much sought-after diary.

When and how remains uncertain. What more he will learn from it, if anything, is also not clear as I suspect he has read it many times during the period that Mary was recording her deepest thoughts and subsequently reporting what she accurately perceived to be break-in incidents for the purposes of spying on her and learning more about her relationship with our deceased president.

But now, JJ has the precious diary in his hands, holding it for the longest time without even opening it, as if its contents, its deepest secrets, are being transmitted to him through some form of spiritual transcendence.

Hard to imagine all that has happened, he finally allows and then retreats back into an increasingly uncharacteristic silence. For a split second, I think I see a tear form in the corner of an eye, but he quickly removes his glasses and wipes it away.

When he notices me staring, he grimaces.

Washington summers, he declares, always so damned humid and sweaty.

Except it is no longer summer in season or spirit in Washington or anywhere in America for that matter. Those times are long gone. Instead, darker days appear to be on the horizon in the form of Vietnam, exacerbating tension between the races. There is no doubt that Lyndon will win next month. But for America, the real question is not about who will win the presidency but what kind of character will imbue the incoming inhabitants of the White House and the people who support our president.

For a good deal of Americans, John Fitzgerald Kennedy represented youth and vitality, what they thought to be great about America. He was perceived, correctly or not, as the golden boy of the future. The kind of representative that America could pride itself in. Educated, erudite, handsome…the attributes are too many to list. In short, a personification of the concept of American exceptionalism. And, yet, behind this façade — the principal character in the popular and evolving portrayal of his time in office as some sort of modern-day Camelot — lay a deeply disturbing reality of that of a dissolute individual who, in so many respects, proved to be a total charade. Too few people knew this and of those that did, most all chose to ignore it until it was too late. Far too late.

Postcript

They are all dead: James Jesus Angleton, Allen Dulles, Richard Helms, LBJ, Ben Bradlee, J. Edgar Hoover, Fidel Castro, the members of the Warren Commission, other key members of the intelligence community from the sixties, and members of the mob associated with various schemes to take out Castro; lastly, but most significantly, Jack Ruby and Lee Harvey Oswald. Each had knowledge not made available to the general public or public investigations, such as the Warren Commission, which they took with them to their graves. As well, though most of the records relating to the work of the Warren Commission are available to the public, some remain sealed under provisions, ironically, of the Kennedy Assassination Records Act.

As for myself, despite all the years that have passed, I remain deeply troubled by what transpired during that period when our elected officials and the people charged with national security often seemed to be more at war with each other rather than engaged in keeping America safe.

Ultimately, I chose to move on. With my mentor no longer pursuing the abhorrent behavior of the late president, my role returned to studying the Trust and the Rote Kapel. The prospect of spending the remaining balance of the precise eleven years required to properly understand — if that was even possible — all the nuances associated with these two elements of past Soviet life was at the very least daunting, if not a complete waste of time.

Also, it quickly became apparent that JJ's need to find closure for his past misjudgments was pushing him to even greater depths of depression and uncertainty with disturbing consequences. At some point, and at whose direction, which is not clear, he began to expand his surreptitious wiretapping practices to include dissidents against the U.S. involvement in Vietnam. How ironic that a man who had bemoaned America's abandonment of those who would oppose the Soviet reign of terror had now turned himself into a self-imposed persecutor of Americans who symbolized the principles of democracy by opposing what they perceived, rightly or wrongly, to be the unauthorized and unlawful prosecution of a foreign war with all the inherent wrongdoing that accompanied it.

Once exposed, JJ was forced to retire, but that merely signified the changing of the guard, not necessarily the practices of the Shadowland.

Principal Characters

CENTRAL INTELLIGENCE AGENCY

James Jesus Angleton, director of counterintelligence, served in WW2 in the Italian underground.

Allen Welsh Dulles, first civilian director of central intelligence, brother of John Foster Dulles, and secretary of state during the two Dwight D. Eisenhower presidential terms.

Richard Bissell, deputy director for plans.

John McCone, director of central intelligence, succeeding Allen Welsh Dulles.

Richard McGarrah Helms, deputy director for plans, later director succeeding John McCone.

Miles Copeland, counterintelligence corps, Strategic Services Unit, father of Stewart Copeland, drummer, member of *The Police* along with Sting and Andy Summers.

Cord Meyer IV, headed the covert action staff of the directorate of plans.

William King "Bill" Harvey, specialized in German and Soviet counterintelligence with the FBI before joining the CIA.

Samuel Halpern, member of Task Force W, partnered with Bill Harvey on Operation Mongoose, charged with ridding Cuba of Fidel Castro.

THE WHITE HOUSE

John Fitzgerald Kennedy, 35th president.

Robert Francis Kennedy, attorney general.

Lyndon Baines Johnson, vice president and 36th president.

Kenneth Patrick O'Donnell, special assistant and appointments secretary to JFK.

Dave Powers, special assistant and assistant appointments secretary.

Ted Sorenson, speech writer.

Arthur Schlesinger Jr., Pulitzer Prize winning historian, special assistant to the president.

McGeorge Bundy, national security advisor to the president, brother of William Bundy, CIA analyst, and foreign affairs advisor to JFK and LBJ.

ALL THE PRESIDENT'S WOMEN

Jacqueline Bouvier Kennedy, first lady.

Caroline Lee Bouvier Canfield Radziwill, Jackie's sister, accompanied JFK during a tour of Germany, England and Ireland when Jackie chose not to travel due to a pregnancy. Estranged from husband, Polish Prince Stanislaw Albrecht 'Stash' Radziwell.

Mary Pinchot Meyer, divorced wife of Cord Meyer, favored mistress of JFK at his death. Her murder, one year later, was never solved.

Judith Exner Campbell, California resident, intimate with JFK and Frank Sinatra, served as the go-between for Kennedy and Chicago mobster Sam Giancana, among others.

Fiddle and Faddle, Priscilla Ware and Jill Cowen, interns at the White House, participated in noon hour pool 'parties' with the president and other staff members.

Marilyn Monroe, Angie Dickenson and Gene Tierney, actresses, all involved with JFK during visits to California. Monroe was also thought to have involvement with Robert Kennedy.

Ellen Rometsch, East German, favorite of many key officials in the Kennedy administration in addition to the president.

THE FBI

Sam Pepich, a long-serving FBI official, who acted as a conduit for the FBI with James Jesus Angleton. It is said that Pepich received an oral report from the CIA's London Station at 9:30 a.m. on Nov. 23 that a warning had been issued to a senior reporter of the Cambridge News just 25 minutes before the assassination of President Kennedy.

J Edger Hoover, director of the FBI for 48 years, credited with modernizing the federal police bureau, also was known to have an extensive trove of files on the activities of notable Americans.

NOTABLES

Peter Lawford, actor, brother-in-law of JFK and RFK. Introduced both to several American actresses, principally Marilyn Monroe, Angie Dickenson, and Gene Tierney.

Harry Lillis 'Bing' Crosby, singer, actor, TV and radio personality. Supporter of President John F. Kennedy.

Timothy Leary, psychologist and advocate of psychedelic drugs. Involved with CIA in the development and usage of LSD (lysergic acid diethylamide). Friend of Mary Meyer, supplied LSD to her and indirectly to JFK.

Daniel Ellsberg, a Pentagon staffer involved in Operation Mongoose during Kennedy's presidency; later exposed

American complicity in Vietnam by releasing Pentagon Papers, of which he was a contributor.

Henry Kissinger, a political scientist, provided expertise on Germany during JFK administration and later served as secretary of state for Richard Nixon.

Ben Bradlee, Washington Post, executive editor overseeing coverage of the Pentagon Papers and Watergate, brother-in-law of Mary Pinchot Meyer.

Mary Jo Kopechne, secretary for Senator George Smathers and room-mate of Nancy Carole Tyler, secretary and lover of Bobby Baker, Washington dealmaker and Vice President Lyndon Baines Johnson confidant. One of the 'boiler room girls' in Bobby Kennedy's ill-fated 1968 presidential campaign. Drowned passenger in car that Senator Ted Kennedy drove off the road on Chappaquiddick Island in 1969.

THE RUSSIANS

Anatoliy Mikhaylovich Golitsyn, a KGB defector, worked in the strategic planning department under the name Ivan Klimov.

Yuri Ivanovich Nosenko, a KGB officer, defected to the U.S. after Golitsyn, who he attempted to cast doubt upon. Confined for three years by the CIA but eventually was deemed a true defector and later worked as a consultant and lecturer for the CIA.

Anatoly Fyodorovich Dobrynin, ambassador to the U.S., 1962-86. Spoke English and French fluently. Key go-between for JFK and Nikita Khrushchev during the Cuban Missile Crisis.

Georgi Nikitovich Bolshakov, a Soviet GRU officer masquerading as a journalist, met with Robert Kennedy on numerous occasions leading up to the Cuban Missile Crisis. Recalled prior to crisis coming to a head.

THE BRITS

Harold Adrian Russell 'Kim' Philby, British intelligence officer, member of the Cambridge Five, a spy ring that divulged British secrets to the Soviet Union during WW 2 and the early stages of Cold War. Defected in 1963. Confidant of James Jesus Angleton in late Forties and Fifties.

Peter Wright, senior officer MI5, British counterintelligence officer. Attempted to out Soviet spies, notably Sir Roger Hollis, director general of MI5 and Sir Anthony Blunt, whose knighthood was later revoked in 1979 on grounds of treason.

Guy Francis de Moncy Burgess, British diplomat and Soviet agent, member of the Cambridge Five spy ring, defected to the Soviet Union in 1951 along with Donald Maclean.

Donald Duart Maclean, British diplomat and Soviet agent, stationed in Paris, London and Washington, member of the Cambridge spy ring, defected with Guy Burgess.

About the Author

JT Grossmith is a retired newspaper editor and publisher with a longstanding interest in American politics, who spends his time equally between Tucson, Arizona and Belleville, Ontario.

www.ingramcontent.com/pod-product-compliance
Lightning Source LLC
Chambersburg PA
CBHW052356030726
47599CB00014B/1086

Nova Albion and The Treasure of Sir Francis Drake

A Real-Life & True Crime Adventure

By

Robert L. Stupack

Copyright © 2024 Robert L. Stupack

All rights reserved.

No part of this publication may be reproduced, distributed, or transmitted in any form or by any means, including photocopying, recording, or other electronic or mechanical methods, without the prior written permission of the publisher, except as permitted by copyright law. For permission requests, contact the author.

Nova Albion and the Treasure of Sir Francis Drake is a work of Creative Nonfiction and all the events described herein are true. However, I have changed certain details as well as the names of most individuals and places mentioned to protect the privacy of others.